Shadow Birds

The Story of a Young Girl During the Partition of India

Anindita Basu

Andrew Benzie Books
Walnut Creek, California

Published by Andrew Benzie Books
www.andrewbenziebooks.com

Copyright © 2019 Anindita Basu. All rights reserved.
www.AninditasWritingRight.blogspot.com

All rights reserved. Except as permitted under the U.S. Copyright Act of 1976, no part of this publication may be reproduced, distributed or transmitted in any form or by any means, or stored in a database or retrieval system without prior written permission of the author.

Printed in the United States of America
First Edition: April 2019

10 9 8 7 6 5 4 3 2 1

Basu, Anindita
Shadow Birds: The Story of a Young Girl During the Partition of India

ISBN 978-1-941713-97-6

Illustrations of the Zentangled bird by Anindita Basu
Cover and book design by Andrew Benzie

In my dreams they come
the shadow birds of my colorful by-gone days
in what hope do they come to wander around my broken cage

—Rabindranath Tagore (translated)

In memory of my mother

Ma,
The last four years of your life you were trapped in bed, paralyzed as a stroke victim. It took away your mobility, but it could not paralyze your memory. You told me stories of your childhood in Mymensingh. You beamed with nostalgic ecstasy, and wilted with helpless agony as you recalled leaving your Motherland to become a refugee. All because of politics and partition.
Living twelve thousand miles away with a window of two weeks vacation each year to spend with you left me with a ton of guilt as your daughter. One day I did admit that to you when I was packing to leave and you said, "Even when I am gone, gone forever, memories will remain. And the stories. You may come and visit them as often as you wish, for as long as you want."
You passed away and I have returned to my normal life in California but often a little girl visits me. She catches me in my quiet hours, while I am driving or when I am washing dishes absentmindedly.
"Who are you?" I ask.
"Khukumoni."
"Where are you from?"
"From the past." She replies.
A lanky little girl of seven or eight years of age, with a missing front tooth, fair as snow, delicate as a fairy, she calls me waving her tiny fingers.
"Come, I'll show you." She takes me by my hand through a lush garden of overgrown bushes where the smell of kul overwhelms the air. She picks one up and puts in my mouth. The jelly like jujube melts under my tongue. Blossoms of shiuli phool underneath our feet feel soft. She picks up a handful and lets them rain. She smashes them between her fingers. The orange stems burst into carnelian hues, filling the air with heavenly smell.
"Magic!" she smiles.
I open my journal and enter another world.
The result is this book. I never had a chance to thank you for telling me your childhood stories. Today I want to give it to you. I close my eyes and visualize that you have come to bless.

CONTENTS

1: 15 August 1947 1
2: Embroidered Quilt 7
3: Best Friend 13
4: Folk Ballads 27
5: Palace of Muktagacha 33
6: Piyari, the Elephant 41
7: Babu 47
8: Sweet Delicacy 53
9: The Dancer's Prayer 63
10: Growing Pain 75
11: A Love Story 81
12: Mightier than a Sword 91
13: Forbidden 97
14: Gramophone 105
15: The Artist Boy 109
16: The Teacher 115
17: The Birth 123
18: The Recovery Act 129
19: Only One Fault 139
20: Sky Lamp 149
21: Shock 159
22: Farewell Motherland 167

1
15 AUGUST 1947

As I spread out the newspaper a caption jumped out—'Murder and Arson Reach New Peak.'

I saw a picture of a long line of people with sad solemn faces, tugging their children, some in bullock carts, some walking in bare feet.

'REFUGEES'—It cried in bold two-inch black letters.

Why is it like this? It should be a day of joy. There should be cheers and bagpipes singing tunes of freedom. There should be processions with the new flag. Today is Independence Day, 15th of August, 1947.

But it was quiet. When I rolled the window shutters to see outside, there was no excitement in my town. Even the birds were not chirping, not a leaf trembling. The sky was filled with solemn grey clouds, rather colorless.

I decided to go to my best friend's house and celebrate. Strapping the sandals on my feet I shouted, "I am going to Padma's house."

"No you are not. Not today." My mother shouted back.

"Why not?" I stamped my foot.

"Because it is not safe. There are several places where there are curfews. Self-imposed curfews. Padma's family—they are Muslims, we are Hindus. You are fourteen years old. My! I expected that you were old enough to understand these things now, Khuku."

"Ma! We are friends. We are best friends since we were six. I am going. I am shocked that you don't understand!" I snapped.

"Khuku! Don't you ever talk to me like that. You are my child. If I say you are not going, you are not going. Go to your room and give it some thought." Ma was clear.

I stomped off to my room, slammed the door and plopped on my bed feeling frustrated that ultimately she won. *She wins. They always win. I never win. They, meaning the rest of the world. I am after all a coward, shaky, wimpy girl who wants to change the world but has no guts.*

The mirror across my bed on the dressing table agreed. That slouchy pose, that beaten up face of mine looked at me. I wiped the tears and took out my diary. My only solace for these kinds of moods, my only weapon to fight my battle.

Querencia (noun)—a place where one feels safe, a place from which one's strength of character is drawn, a place where one feels at home. That is what came out of my pen today on my journal and stared at me.

March 15, 2003

The name of the place was Mymensingh, pronounced as my men sing. This was where I was born. This was where I grew up. This was my motherland, my home. But I cannot go home. No, not anymore, not without permission and a visa. It is in a different country today.

It is on the map of Bangladesh. When I was born, the district of Mymensingh was part of undivided India. In 1947, when India got her freedom from the British, it was dissected into two nations: India (or Hindustan) and Pakistan. West of India, turned into West Pakistan, east of India, East Pakistan. We fell on the East Pakistan side. Much later, in 1971, East Pakistan became a sovereign nation, Bangladesh.

After the partition of 1947, many Hindu families who lived in the East Pakistan part moved west to India, many Muslim families who lived in India moved to Pakistan. It was the largest migration in human history. Millions of Hindu, Sikh and Muslim families became homeless because of this partition. We were one of them.

My Mymensingh, as I remember her, *was* filled with songs and notes of happy melodies. Smell of *shiuli phool, a* tiny white flower with a carnelian orange center covered the whole portico of our home. In autumn it made a large circle of dropped blossoms, like a white welcome *galicha*. That heavenly smell fills me, unaltered, even after all these sixty years.

I am stuck in bed now after the stroke. When I turn to my side, a door opens up on the white wall beside my bed. The door to my memory lane.

If I look closely, I can see lines and scribbles on that white-washed wall, images of shadow birds. Shadows of my rainbow days of the bygone years that flew away and I could hold no more. Now they hop around my broken cage. I look at their dance with quiet awe.

Then from deep down somewhere a haze arises. Mist of silence. And then?

I hear someone calling my childhood nickname… Khu-ku-moni.

Mymensingh 1941

It had been a peaceful morning until the newspaper came.

I was busy discovering all kinds of magic in our garden that early spring day. Flower pots on the entry steps were brimming with bursts of red hibiscus and the white star jasmine crept up the columns and entangled my swing on the porch. New leaves, as large as the elephant's ears, with the darkest bottle green shade and tiny dots shot up from the planter box. I thought the garden fairy must have visited at night and painted those red and white dots on the leaves with sandalwood paste.

Our ivory color brick house had curved doorways with dark green wooden shutters and through the arched stained glass windows yellow, orange and red lights flooded and reflected on the floor. I was playing hopscotch with the patterns and then chasing a tiny white butterfly, entered the garden. Babu, my father, was weeding kneeled down close to the ground with his back toward me. Sweat drops glistened on his almost bald head. I tip-toed and quickly covered his eyes from behind with my little hands. His glasses flung. He turned.

"You! Aren't you cold, little one?" He wrapped me with his soft woolen shawl and picked me up. I put my head on his shoulder. Soap, soil, sweat made up my daddy-smell. No one in the whole world smelled the same.

"What are you doing?" I asked him.

He put me down. "Look, these are the new growth of the seeds we had planted the other day, but these are no good, just weeds." He tried to give me a lesson in gardening. But I turned away, I heard the garden latch clank.

It was Jasimuddin, our gardener, helper, a caretaker, a person whom I saw as my older brother and addressed as Jasim-da (brother Jasim). He was a tall, lanky man with a black beard, and always with a smile on his face.

Jasim-da, in a grey, long kurta and his usual black *Mussulman Tupi* (Muslim cap) was coming with the morning paper in his hand like he did every day. I ran to him.

"Jasim-da, where is the thing you promised to bring?"

"Wait, little sister." He smiled and handed the newspaper to my father.

I knew Babu would ask for his morning cup of tea now and go inside. This would be the end of the garden session for this morning. But today it was different. Babu took the newspaper and stretched it out. His brows knitted. His face looked disturbed. "What?" he murmured to himself and sat down on the step. He did not go inside, nor did he ask for his tea. Something was wrong.

"What is it Babu?" I asked. He closed his eyes, not sure how to explain it to a seven-year-old child and turned to Jasimuddin.

"The Lahore Resolution is passed. Passed on March 24."

"What does that mean, Sir?" Jasim-da gazed at his face.

"It means that the Muslim majority areas are asking for a separate place. Areas in the west of India like Lahore, Karachi, and in the east, Bengal do not want to be part of Hindustan, India, even when the British give us freedom."

"Then what will happen Sir?" Jasimuddin asked.

"I don't know. I don't know how we can solve it, Jasim." Babu looked into his face.

Jasimuddim lowered his eyes looking at the ground, his hands folded, not sure how to respond.

I went to him and whispered in his ear, "Jasim-da, aren't you going to ask permission for the puppy now, please?"

"It's not a good day, little sister," he mumbled back with sad eyes.

2
EMBROIDERED QUILT

The small village still gazes at the faraway one
Whispering in silence, tears in eyes.
Dry fields lie in between
Cracked, baked in the hot sun.
Ruthless peasants cut the paddies that cloaked the earth
And take them to some far between land
That we do not know.

—Poet Jasimuddin 1920-1976
Translated from Nokshi Kanthar Maath

I was an only child. No siblings, no playmates to fool around with. My only companion was my blanket. My security blanket. I called it, my *nokshi kantha*. Elderly relatives used to tell stories that when I was a child, I carried that quilt everywhere, sweeping the whole universe. It was catastrophic to part with it. My parents had a hard time washing or cleaning it. I don't remember that. All I remember is, what a sense of security it gave me—that little piece of rag.

"Your mother made it even before you were born. With the thread of her colorful saris, she embroidered the designs, these vines of hope design." Baroma, my aunt, pointed to the vines, sliding her fingers over the leaves of the pattern.

I picked it up and brushed it against my cheek, "Soft! How come it is so soft?" I'd ask.

"The quilt is made with your father's old cotton dhotis that were washed and washed several times and became so soft," she replied.

No wonder it was so special; it had the smell of Babu and the vines-of-hope designs of my ma's hands. My life started wrapped in that special blanket.

When I was little, I vividly remember playing with the designs on the quilt. My fingers would hop with the seams of the embroidery patterns where the blue stitches ran up to get lost in the green field, passing the orange French knot flowers. Run, run, run, way up to the indigo tiny triangle appliqués. They were like the hillocks of the Sushong Hills which I could see from my window. Then I'd find tiny maroon squares and rectangles just like the red tile roof-tops of the huts beneath the hills. Hop with the orange lazy daisy chain stitches that spiraled into the center, like the sun, and then escape behind the green vines. Oh, how it found its way to the tan border at the end. It was the same ginger hue of the Brahmaputra River. Does the orange spiral want to take a dip in that ginger-tan water? I wondered.

I felt like a free white breasted kite bird flying in the wide open sky and then dropping on the soft plushness of the *nokshi kantha*.

That blanket hugged me.

*   *   *

My parents were protective. Rather overprotective. They thought I was like a delicate baby sparrow, or a fragile glass doll, who might break very easily. This tiny, thin, delicate child had to be kept wrapped in cotton balls, away from all outside trouble. Going to friends' houses was not allowed. Instead, why don't they come here?

When my friends came, they were treated like grown-ups, with delicious puffed *loochi* (fried dough) and *monda* (the famous sweet meat of Mymensingh) in silver platters, then they were escorted home in one of our four-wheeled horse drawn phaetons. I thought my friends who came from normal middle-class families felt most awkward with all this aristocratic fuss, because they never came to play again.

I learned to play alone, made a world of my own.

*   *   *

Clutching my father's finger as tight as I could, I went to start my new school.

Bidyamoyee Girls' School was very big. The two-storied red brick building was almost a block long with a large playground. Greystone walls guarding all around, were even taller than my father. A massive iron gate threatened with a loud clank as the shackles closed the doors when the bell rang.

After my father left I felt lost. *What is this strange place? Where are all the girls going following a line?* That is when I met a lady. She looked robust and strong and she stared at me through a pair of round spectacles. I froze.

"Why are you standing here? Don't you know where to go?"

I shook my head.

"Okay, I'll show you. You are the new student." Her voice was deep, husky, almost like that of a man. "No fear, just follow me." Her voice mellowed.

I had heard that the headmistress of this school could make 'the cow and the tiger drink from the same bank.' What does that mean Babu, I asked my father and came to learn that it was a proverb in Bengali meaning she is very strict, with a strong personality and does not tolerate nonsense. I understood this must be the headmistress who had that reputation.

"Come here, girl, this is your new class."

She did not ask my name or anything more, but the way she touched my shoulder gently and pushed me with a kind smile, I had a feeling that everything would be fine.

An elderly man with a bald head and a ruler in his hand was the teacher. He tried to keep the students in order, screaming louder than the students he accused. Some giggled. He clarified he would not accept such silliness. On the big blackboard he wrote H U T and all the girls shouted 'hut.' He wrote B U T and everyone shouted 'but.' In a nasal tone he said, "Well, B U T is but, H U T is hut now who can tell me what P U T will be? No shouting, raise your hand."

Many students raised their hands, I did too. I knew the answer to this tricky question. He looked at me,

"You!" As soon as I stood up to answer, he furiously yelled, "Who asked you, hmm?" and glared at me with utter disgust. He shocked me. I felt a lump in my throat. No one had ever talked to me like that, never scolded me in such a rude tone, not even my own parents. I tried to gulp my embarrassment and hold the tears that were threatening to roll down my face.

I looked around. The other girls were grinning. One of them could not hide it and when our eyes met she quickly covered her two-front-teeth-missing giggle.

That day on my way back home, I found that this girl was sitting next to me in the school bus. The bus took a long route. Through the *City bazzar, Gol Pukur, Durga bari, Kesto Pukur Road,* across the riverside, around the *Pocha Pukur*—Rotten Lake it would reach the *Station Road*. Reading the names of the streets with the rocking motion of the vehicle, I dozed off.

Suddenly I heard someone whispering in my ear, "A*yee*, I am Padma, what's your name?"—that two-front-teeth-missing girl.

"Khukumoni." I replied half asleep. She grabbed my hand. "Mine too. Khuku. But that's my nickname."

That is a very common Bengali nickname, meaning, precious little girl.

She turned her head and checked around, then with wide eyes whispered again, "I must tell you something. There are naughty girls here. You'll find out yourself, I need not point. They tie the ribbons of your braids with the back of the seat when you fall asleep and then get off the bus before you do. You would not know... and when it is your time to get down, you are stuck. The driver gets cross when you are late and..and..." Saying she untied the knots of the ribbon from my braid that was carefully tied with the wooden bar of the back seat. I felt so thankful. Then she continued:

"And Hori babu sir, the English teacher who scolded you today is a little cross-eyed, you know. Sometimes it is confusing who he is really looking at. You'll get used to it soon. Don't worry too much about that." She smiled.

At this point the bus stalled. There was a procession going. Lots of men with *tupi* on their heads and red *jhandhas* were shouting '*Inquilub Zindabad*'! The placards on their hands read—we want justice.

I overheard the driver explaining it to a senior student that there was a Muslim athlete who brought a lot of pride to us all but the Hindus refused him when he went to drink the water from a tube well that the Hindu community only used. The Muslims were angry that the Hindus cheered when he brought the trophy but refused to let him touch their water. That was what this protest was for. That was why we were in the middle of a traffic jam.

"That's not nice. It must be hurtful to the Muslim boxer who won the trophy," commented the older girl.

My new friend, Padma, asked me, "Are you Muslim Khukumoni? I am."

"I don't think so." I shook my head.

"Never mind. Now, we'll have more time to chat. If I invite, will you come to our house to play?"

3

BEST FRIEND

To commemorate our friendship, especially since our nicknames were also the same, Padma and I decided to have a best friend namesake celebration.

We made some ceremonial designs with a stick on the dirt, a tic-tac-toe frame with hearts and circles drawn here and there and decided to call each other 'Soi,' which meant special friend. But it had to be a secret. No one else should know about our *Soi* thing. Then my friend stated that we must tell each other a secret of our lives, which we had never told any one and will never do in the future. There was great responsibility involved in this decision. "You must keep it a secret and never ever tell your *soi's* secret to anyone. Agree?"

"But dear Soi what if I don't have a secret? I really don't." I pouted.

"Well, I can wait. Just tell it when you have one, someday."

"Do you have one, dear Soi?" I asked.

"Yes. But remember the deal? It is hard keeping it all to yourself. It needs a very strong mind."

"What if I fail?" I pleaded.

"That is a betrayal. Real bad thing will happen then. So bad you can't even imagine. One will be seriously hurt. Either you or me. One will. No choice. Now, can you handle?"

I took a deep breath, "Yes. You can trust me. I am strong. I can handle that."

"Okay, then. Cross your heart and say this with me." She muttered something that I repeated after. Then she cupped her hands onto my ear and whispered her secret.

*   *   *

I had never realized that it would be so hard to digest Padma's secret. The more I prayed for strength, the more I wanted to forget it, it came right back to me like a boomerang. It chased me wherever I went, like an annoying mosquito buzzing in my ear. I felt bloated with that secret as if it was growing bigger and bigger inside me and would burst out and kill me. It had been three days I kept it all to myself but I couldn't take anymore.

One day I decided that I will tell it to my mother. I hid nothing from her. And telling her does not count. She is just Ma. I am not blabbing it in our lunchroom or so.

The winter afternoon sun cast a warm glow on the veranda. We were basking in that long rectangle of light. Ma was braiding my hair.

All of a sudden I blurted out,

" You know Ma, my friend Padma… she is actually an orphan. An abandoned child by the real parents. The maidservant found the baby wrapped in a dirty old rag near a dustbin. The maid brought her to Padma's mother. Her mom did not have any girls before, only two sons, so when the maid showed her the child she felt sorry for the baby, and picked her up with pity. Padma's older brother told her this story. He said, 'Otherwise did you ever see anyone in our family with both teeth missing in the front? You are clearly not from our family. You came as an orphan. We just took pity on you. And that is why we named you Padma (Lotus), as it grows in the middle of mud. See that?'… But Ma, dear Ma, please don't tell it to anybody… please… please." I held my hands together, praying to her.

Ma kept silent. Nonchalant. Her indifference shocked me. After a while she muttered, "Keep your head straight, my you have tangles," and brushed my hair with more vigor, battling with the tangles.

I cried out: "You are mean. Mean to my hair and my friend. Leave me alone... and don't you have any feelings for Padma?" I was choked with tears.

She laughed instead. "All gibberish. Padma has the same features as her dad, the same eyes, same chin. There is a saying in Bengali—a face like dad, life won't be sad... and she got her mom's complexion. Rather, I find the brother... a monkey."

I jumped up. "Wow! Let me go tell her." I was so happy.

"Where are you heading my child? Just calm down. Can't you see it is dark outside?"

Yes, indeed. The lamp-men were lighting the street lamps. It was a new moon night. Outside was dark. Conches blew from faraway houses, the ritual for greeting the evening, shoving away the evil spirits.

I felt disappointed that I could not go tell it to my friend. Next morning I saw something that cheered me up. The suitcases were out. The big metal trunk was open. They were dusted and cleaned, ready to be packed. There were baskets of goodies and a big box full of sweets, *Dhakai bakharkhani*, the special dessert from Dhaka. This special sweet dish is a circle of about six inches, made of something crisp and sweet with an aroma of fresh ghee!

"Ma, are we going to Grandpa's house?" I ran and hugged her tight. This was my favorite treat. No school, no homework. All my cousins, my peers, my friends would be there. I could do whatever I wanted and Ma would not be able to scold, even get a hold of me. Oh, what fun!

The next day we boarded the train to Bataspur. Jasimuddin, our loyal, servant escorted Ma and me as Babu could not go. Women in those days did not travel without a male escort.

The train left Mymensingh station and picked up speed—*jhik jhik jhik*.

I fancied rhyming-Tell me o dear train, how far is Grandpa's terrain?

A piercing shrill of the whistle and a gush of smoke replied—

Quooo! Grandfather's home is far away Khukumoni, it is not quick. Quooo jhik jhik.

SHADOW BIRDS

Up the hill, down the valley, over the bridge, the train rumbled with a monotonous *dok-a-dok, dok-a-dok* sing-song rhythm. Way down below the ginger-colored Brahmaputra River was flowing. At the bank, two fishermen flung their nets, busy in their dinghy boats. In the middle of the river, a large *bazra* sailed leisurely in royal style. Probably it was traveling to or from Kolkata or Rangoon, filled with precious goods.

*   *   *

"Come, Khuku, this time we have to ride a bullock cart. They have no *tonga* at this hour in the station." Jasim da stretched his hands.

Bataspur *gram,* our destination, was a quaint little village, not so busy like Mymensingh town. There was a small opening with curtain in the bullock cart. I moved the curtain and found we were in a jungle. Light filtered through dense tropical plants, wind murmured through the leaves.

Tall *supari trees* bordered the sides of the road. First, I thought they were palm or coconut trees, but no, their leaves were much daintier and thin. Mango groves filled my senses and the jackfruits, almost half my size hung in clusters. Their strong, pungent, smell overwhelmed my urban taste. But I loved the jujube. We called them k*ul.* I could easily reach them. They were hanging from bushes. When they were ripe they tasted like jelly inside a fruit. Ma made chutney with them.

The cart moved at a snail's pace with a monotonous grinding clang, the bullocks groaned whining moos. Bugs buzzed and I wondered *How far is Grandpa's home?*

We crossed many ponds, and lakes, brooks and bridges and then the cart slowed down as we entered the estate.

People from all over came to greet us. They carried our luggage and hustled to give us the best room. My cousins swarmed around me as if I were the queen bee. They were glad to oblige me with coconut water. One hurried to bring the green coconut, showing off his skill in cutting the opening with a scythe, the other brought a glass.

The girls brushed their fingers on my satin frock which was very different from the tightly wrapped spun cotton saris they wore. Village children ran in bare feet. They stared at my toes dressed with beautiful leather sandals. It impressed me that they were adoring my urban looks, my unique style.

A chubby looking boy came forward.

"I'll show you around. You call me Manik da (big brother Manik) as I am older than you. How old are you Khuku?"

"Eight, almost, nine." I replied.

"Really! I thought you were six, at the most seven." The moon face boy sniggered. That put me in a bad mood.

"Look, this is where we live. And that one, see that yellow thatched-roof house, that is our family's quarter." I understood that each of my grandfather's sons had a quarter for his individual family. The houses were quite modest, not as beautiful as our house in Mymensingh. There were several such quarters scattered in the grand estate.

"This is our communal kitchen where all the food is cooked." He proceeded to the gigantic kitchen where food for over hundred people was cooked each day.

"Then again, the main kitchen has three separate sections." He added.

"How come there are three different sections?" I wondered.

"The one over there is just for the temple. Only special people can cook that food. You don't know all these things?" He squinted his eyes spinning a sling on his finger.

"And this is where they cook vegetarian food," he led us to a room where a group of ladies was hustling with all kinds of food preparation. They were all wearing white saris, some were old in age, some quite young. But they all were widows. That is why they wore white clothes, no jewelry or adoration, and they ate only vegetarian food.

"Come, taste this *naru*. We just made it with fresh coconut from our garden and the new molasses. Very good, *na*?" An aunt gave each of us a sweet coconut ball that was yummy.

SHADOW BIRDS

The nonvegetarian kitchen was where the real activity took place. Several cooks and their helpers were busy cooking. Huge cauldrons and canteens were cooking delicious dishes on three gigantic clay *unun* (oven). They were so high that one of the cooks picked me up to show what was happening. I saw fish simmering in a red pungent sauce of garlic, ginger, turmeric, cardamom, cinnamon, tomatoes, green chillies and what not.

I had heard the description of heaven and the hell at one time. In heaven, everything was serene and peaceful, but in hell there was a huge cauldron on a huge fire pit. If you were bad or naughty you were put in that cauldron that would cook you up with all your bad karma. That image came to my mind. I shivered to see the condition of the fish and decided I'd not be eating that thing.

The fat cook with almost no chin joked, "Are you hungry?"

I was just relieved that he put me down on the ground.

"You look scared and nervous, are you?" scoffed Manik.

"Wimpy woman! Just stay with me. Listen to what I say, follow me and you'll be fine." He added.

"I am not wimpy, I am strong." I crossed my brows.

"Look at her wrists, like pencils. Want to have a fist fight? Hey all, look at her ears, like our baby elephant's." He flapped my ears and grinned.

I could feel my cheeks burning, my eyes scorching. I stomped out of the group, marched to my room, grabbed a book and sat under a tree.

The children were quite astonished to see such a reaction. No fight, no crying, just grab a book and quit the group! They did not leave me alone and they kept following me like a swarm of bugs.

"Let's go to the *Bahir Mahal*. That is the office, where the men work." Mira pulled my frock. Mira was a little older than me but a head taller and much bigger. She had long, thick hair which she knotted into a tight bun at the top of her head. It often got untied and she fixed it jerking her head and letting all that hair fall in front of her face. She quickly wrapped it into her palm and pushed it to form a bun with an amazing skill that I had only seen in grown ups.

Through the windows, we saw that in a fairly large room there was a big divan like furniture that occupied the whole room. Low in height, rectangular in shape, this divan like furniture was draped with a white cotton bedspread. It was the one and only thing in the room, with many cushions and pillows thrown on it. The pillows were cylindrical, some square, covered with red velvet and gold-colored strings, and some just normal rectangular ones. Our uncles and other men were sitting on this big *farash,* that is the name of this furniture piece, Mira taught. Some stretched out with a pillow under the neck, some under their elbows. Two men were playing a game and having an argument. One grabbed the coins that were scattered in front and the other man was screaming. I learned that the game was called *pasha.*

Only one man, with a lens on one eye, was seriously working with some numbers on his ledger. He scratched his head and shuffled the notebook and then stared in space with a pen tucked behind his ear. Poor man, probably was stuck with his calculation. He reminded me of my father.

"We are the zaminders and our responsibility is to collect taxes from our *praja,* (subjects), and pay that money to the British Raj." Manik decided to educate me how the system worked.

"The land is ours, I mean our grandfather's, and his heirs, like us, yours too Khuku." After a pause he started, "we let the common people work on our land, like fishermen may fish in our ponds, farmers plow our land, but for that they must pay us the tax. See that boy, Kanu," he pointed to a boy, "his father is a *praja.* He and his family farm on our land. They are not Brahmin. We are. You too, Khuku." Manik was trying to be my friend.

I looked at Kanu, a thin fellow with ebony dark complexion, wearing a small piece of loincloth up to his knees. His upper body was bare, showing his bony ribs that were more pathetic than mine.

"Manik da, I dug the hole and found no coins growing like you said. You said that they will grow like potato plants that multiply under the ground. But my coins are not growing. And the ones I planted before, are gone too." Kanu whined in a feeble voice.

"What! Did you dig them up already?" Manik barked with his brows knitted.

"Didn't I tell you just to squish each coin every day and only water them, not to disturb the soil? Didn't I? You bad boy!" he growled.

Kanu sniffled, wiping his eyes. Manik mellowed, "It takes time, my friend. Have patience and faith." He put an arm on Kanu's shoulder.

Mira rolled her eyes. She explained whispering to me that Manik convinced Kanu that if he planted money under the ground and watered it, it would multiply and Kanu's family would be well off one day. There would be no poverty in their house. The goddess Lakshmi would come and bring abundance.

Mira drew Kanu aside. "Kanu, you must stop stealing money. Where are you getting them from?"

"From the earthen pot, my mother keeps next to the Goddess Lakshmi, in our praying altar." He answered.

"Stop that. Stop that Kanu. That is bad. Not only your mother and father will be angry with you if they know, but Mother Lakshmi also will never ever forgive you for stealing. Listen, money never grows under the ground like that. Promise you'll stop?" Mira looked at him straight. The poor boy nodded, "Okay, I'll stop."

*   *   *

We heard a big commotion near the Bahir Mahal. A fat man with a protruded belly was beating up a small scrawny fellow.

"You should have known better. It is a big deal, now someone's caste is at stake. If a Hindu touches or smokes from the same pipe that a *Mussulman* had used, he loses his good caste, his class, don't you know these basic things? Why did you touch it? Who asked you?" He shouted.

The gawky, thin man brushed his palms against each other. With teary eyes he looked up praying, *"Ebarkar moto maap kore din, karta."*

"You've done something sinful, very bad. Something very serious. I don't know even charging you fines can clear what you have done." The fat man with thick lips pouted.

"I meant no harm, *huzur*. Just wanted to clean them." The accused fellow tried to apologize.

"*Chup!* Shut up. Not a single word. Just go. Get lost." The fat man jerked his face and stomped off.

*   *   *

"Come, I'll show you something very interesting." Manik led us to check out where the drama began. I saw some vessels with long pipes on various shelves. They looked interesting.

"Hookah!" His eyes shone.

Looking closely I noticed that there were three different shelves and the so-called hookahs were different in styles indeed.

Some were made with brass with elaborate designs of flowers and vines etched on the bottom pot. A spherical pot was joined with a long neck. It had a pipe attached to it. On another shelf, there were some that had several smaller pots attached to a long neck and a pipe. At the lowest shelf, the hookahs were not at all fancy looking. They were just clay pots with pipes on the top. The only thing common was that all of them had pipes attached to some kind of pots.

Manik took one down carefully from the highest shelf, the most elaborate, beautiful one.

"These are only for the Brahmins." He pointed to the highest shelf and inhaled, smoking through the pipe. A sweet smell of tobacco emerged and it made a funny *ghuruk-ghuruk* sound. He gave a proud smile and extended the pipe to me.

"Want to try?"

Mira stepped forward, "No Khuku, don't. Women don't smoke."

"Yes, because they are wimpy." Manik mocked.

"No, because we choose not to." Mira barked back.

"I choose not to, and I am strong." I joined her, stomping my feet, hands on my waist.

Manik picked up my wrists and played with my ears, "Pencil wrist, pencil wrist. Flappy ears!" He teased. Tears rolled down my cheeks.

"Come, come with me." Mira touched my shoulder and shoved Manik away.

"Leave us alone. You have no idea what women can do. Did you ever hear the name *Jhansir Rani*, Manik?" She bellowed. Mira's frizzy, curly hair came off the bun she knotted on the top. Now they were flying, like flames, framing her heart-shaped face. Her big eyes shone wide. With flaring nostrils she looked like Ma Durga, ready to perish the demon.

She grabbed my hand and took me to Didi, who was feeding her infant.

"Didi, can you please tell us the story of *Jhansir Rani*, one more time. Please. You told us one day it was a woman, the queen of Jhansi who was the pioneer to rebel against the British Raj. She was one of the first ones, who was considered the most dangerous, the most courageous and the strongest of all. She was the fiercest first who stood up for wrongdoing… didn't you ? Tell us that story one more time, please."

Didi smiled. She patted the back of her baby with gentle strokes while pacing back and forth, then started:

"'*Mei Jhansi nehi dungi!*' said the queen of Jhansi, to the British, meaning I will not give up Jhansi."

"Long ago, a hundred years from now, there lived a queen in a place named Jhansi. Her people lovingly called her Mani as her real name was Manikarnika, meaning a piece of gem, and a gem she was. She was also known by Lakhmi Bai. She lost her mom when she was only four. Her father brought her up not as a docile, domestic daughter, but like a strong son. Mani, learned how to read and write and at the same time had formal training in martial art, fencing, archery, horse riding." Didi nodded her head as it was quite amazing news for us to hear that women could take such lessons even hundred years ago. Mira sat closer to me. I held her hand.

Didi continued, "She was married to the king of Jhansi but lost her husband too early, within a few years. When the king died, the British wanted to take over Jhansi, offering her a meager pension. The British denied the kingship to their adopted son, who was still a child, and laughed that the queen wanted to rule. The queen wrote a petition to the Governor-general, sent an envoy to London to plead her case, but the British denied."

"It was not easy for a woman to be the head of a state in those days, but the Rani succeeded. All her people loved her and said they'd support her in her decisions. They assured that if the British came to attack they'd lay down their lives to defend Jhansi. The Rani inspired the women to join the army and take an active role in defending their homeland. She offered them military training to become strong and resourceful."

"One day the British attacked Jhansi with a huge army equipped with powerful cannons. With the help of traitors, they entered the fort at night in an overwhelming number. The Rani went underground. The British were disappointed that they couldn't catch her."

At this point Mira drew even closer to Didi, "And, and what happened, Didi?"

Didi cackled, "You have heard this story so many times, Mira." She shook her head and gently laid the baby as the baby had fallen asleep.

"The British became frustrated not finding the queen, so they took out their wrath burning the excellent library, ransacking the palace, murdering the Rani's main followers. They killed common people, even innocent children, and women."

"But the Queen of Jhansi was determined, *'Mei Jhansi nehi dungi.'* She fought the British, she'd not surrender. Tying her baby on her back, swords in both hands she slashed, and whipped and thrashed as severely as she could. Dressed like an army man she fought, and fought. No one could recognize her as a woman. It was the fiercest, bloodiest battle ever fought on Indian soil. For two weeks the fight continued until…" Didi stopped in the middle of the sentence to rock the baby as she fussed. We felt that we were transported in a different era. We were at the battlefield with the queen. Now back to reality, Mira became impatient. She wanted to help Didi, at the same time listen to the rest of the story.

"And… and then, Didi?" Mira held her chin up.

"The queen lost. She fell off the horse and bled severely. No one knew except her loyal servant. The queen had a wish, and this servant was aware of her last wish. 'Don't let a British ever touch me.' So when she died the servant took her body quietly to a hermit who did her last ritual, at the burning pyre."

"Jhansir Rani will remain in history as the symbol of resistance to the British Raj, as the fiercest, most dangerous and most courageous of all the rebels. She will also live in our heart forever to remind each girl in India that women are powerful and they do not give up easily," Didi concluded.

"Mei Jhansi nehi dungi" Mira exclaimed and I repeated after her, energized with enormous vim and vigor.

*　　　*　　　*

The afternoon passed swiftly, and right before the sundown there was a big commotion. It was time for arranging and cleaning the lanterns, and lamps and getting them ready for the night as there was no electricity in the village.

Little by little sunlight faded until a charcoal black darkness engulfed the little community. Insects buzzed *zee-zee-zeee*. Frogs joined them with their *ganor gang-ganor gang* and the jackals added *awhooooo* as the grand finale.

If you had the guts to go out on a new moon night you'd see millions of stars, the Milky Way. If Babu were here, he would point to the Big Dipper, *Saptarshi*, the constellation of the seven sages. *Otri, Ongira, Pulaho, Pulasto, Ketu, Boshito and Marich* are their names. He'd make sure that I knew them by heart. He'd show me *Kalpurush*, the Orion with his hanging sword and the three tiny stars on his belt. One of them was called *Krittika*. Babu told me that *Chandra*, the Moon, had twenty-eight wives scattered all over the celestial constellations and *Krittika* was one of those wives. "But look there, the reddish star *Rohini*, she is the most beloved one of Chandra. Chandra and Rohini, are like Romeo and Juliet in Hindu astrology," he told me.

But Babu was not here this time, so I curled up with my cousins and cuddled under the warm comforter and listened to Didi's stories.

Didi, recently married and now living in Kolkata with her in-laws had just come to visit and brought lots of gifts for us. She had handed us pretty packets and inside there were celluloid toys and bone china dolls that were sold in Kolkata. We had no idea that such wonderful toys existed.

She told us how in Christmas the city was all decked up with lights and paper lanterns. The Saint Paul Cathedral was lit with beautiful lights and the Park Street adorned with garlands of lights. *Saheb, Mem* (white men and women) dressed in beautiful gowns and suits went hand in hand to the finest bakeries, like Firpo and Flurry's. Oh the smell of those goodies!

At midnight Father Christmas came and left presents for the children in their stockings while they were sleeping and the church bell chimed ding-dong-ding-dong to celebrate baby Jesus' birthday. It was so magical.

Shovan, who was three years younger than me, asked, "How could Father Christmas know who have hung their socks?"

Mira replied, "You got to be a *Kiristian* (Christian). Father Christmas does not come to Hindu children. So never mind, you'd not make it."

"What is being a *Kiristian*? I'd rather be that." he scowled.

"Never say that, Shovan. That is giving up your religion. The worst thing that can happen to you. Don't you see there is so much problem with this religion business, the Hindu- Muslim thing?"

"What is a religion?" he wondered with wide eyes.

"Oh, my! Never mind. It is very late. I want you all to close eyes and no talking at all." Didi warned us and blew out the clay lamp.

With my eyes closed, I could see Kolkata, the beautiful, big city, full of light, filled with the smell of vanilla sweet cakes and happy children walking with their parents, holding Christmas gifts in their hands.

Oh God, whoever you are, Jesus, or Krishna or Allah, please, please please grant me just one wish. Take me to Kolkata just once in my life. I prayed folding my hands.

Then I fell into a deep sleep.

4
FOLK BALLADS

Three bullock carts full of people came to the village. They sang folk songs. We came to know that they were going to perform a drama in the evening. These ballad people were known to us as *jatradol*.

They performed right in our courtyard putting up a fake stage with no curtains or light accents other than lanterns and petromax lamps. But we looked forward to it anxiously, any way. They would perform from the epic *Ramayana*.

King Dasharath is sad because he has everything but no heirs. He has three beautiful queens but none could give him a son. Then one day Queen Kaikeyi with the help of a shrewd maidservant, Manthara, finds a magic potion that promises to bring forth royal children. The queen shares it with the other two queens too and lo and behold they all get pregnant soon enough. The eldest queen Kaushalya gives birth to Ram, Kaikeyi to Bharat and the youngest queen, Sumitra, a twin—Lakhan and Shatrugna.

King Dasharath is overjoyed. "What can I give you my dear queen, Kaikeyi? You have given me the most precious gift. Fatherhood. I am now the father of four wonderful sons."

"I wish two blessings from you, your majesty, but may I claim them later?" she requests. The King feels generous and agrees. "Tell me when you are ready, no hurry, dear queen. It will be granted whenever you utter it." The King kisses her hand.

King Dasharath has approached old age. He wants to retire giving the throne and the responsibility to his eldest son, Ram, who has recently been married to the loveliest bride Sita, the daughter of Mother Earth.

The palace is decorated with flowers, the royal kitchen is filled with the aroma of good food, the whole kingdom is ready to celebrate the joyous crowning ceremony of Prince Ram.

This is when that cunning maidservant Manthara enters the stage, tiptoes with her hunchback and whispers to queen Kaikeyi curling up her nose, "What is there for you if Ram becomes the king? Your son deserves to be the one. This is your time to claim those wishes."

Kaikeyi goes to King Dasharath. "Your Majesty, do you remember the wishes you promised me years ago? Would you be able to keep them if I ask now?"

"Of course, Queen. A promise is a promise and when it comes from me it is a royal promise. Just say it."

"Well, then my first one is, not Ram, but Bharat, my son shall be the king and my second one is, Ram should be banished from the kingdom to the deep jungle and not come back until fourteen years pass. After that he may be the ruler and get your throne."

Hearing this King Dasharath faints. But the royal promise has to be kept. So, Ram goes in exile to the deep forest of Chitrakoot with his bride Sita. Lakhan could not tolerate it, so he follows them too.

In the jungle a *rakshashi* (demon in disguise of a beautiful maiden), Surpanakha, seduces Ram. Lakhan rescues him and insults her. Her brother, the mighty king of the Far East, Ravan decides to take revenge. He, disguised as a beggar comes to Sita and asks for alms while she is alone in the cottage. Ravan kidnaps Sita and takes her to the island of Lanka surrounded by the ocean (modern Sri Lanka) in his flying chariot (modern day airplane) led by the gigantic bird Garuda.

This part of the epic, Ramayan was what the folk dramatics were playing that day. Men acted out women's role putting padding on their breasts and wearing long, wigs. With red ink they colored their lips that were smoking cheap *bidis* a few minutes ago. But we did not care.

We, with our aunts and cousins, dressed in our best outfits, saris and jewelry, came to grace our own courtyard as if we were going to see some grand opera. The whole village came too to see the performance.

When Dasharath fell down, heart broken at Kaikeyi's cruelty, the audience was shaken. They cried—*Ish ish!*

Mira told me the rest of the story during the break.

Ravan holds Sita captive in Lanka, asking for her hands. Sita revolts. She protests even living and sleeping under the same roof with him. Sita resides in the palace garden, where she pines for her beloved Ram and contemplates suicide. One day the monkey warrior Hanuman visits her. He shows Ram's signet ring. Understanding Sita's situation he assures that her purity will burn Ravan to ashes. Thus she can escape. But Sita knows that such showing off her woman power is not virtuous.

Ram with the help of Hanuman and the army of monkey warriors wins the battle, kills Ravan and rescues Sita. When they go back to his kingdom Ayodhya Sita's chastity is questioned. Questioned by Ram too. Sita has to go through a fire test.

Sita enters the funeral pyre but comes out unchanged, unburned, like a statue of gold. Ram embraces her as his queen and they lived happily until he hears a common launderer bad mouthing Sita regarding her purity. Ram reacts. Instead of punishing the gossiper, he banishes his pregnant wife Sita to the forest. Sita finds refuge in sage Valmiki's home where she gives birth to her twin sons, Lab and Kush. Fourteen years later Ram finds them out as his sons and regards them as his princes. He recognizes Sita too, but does not welcome her as his queen. Heartbroken, Sita lies down on the ground praying, 'If you are truly my Mother then take me back to your womb.' Mother Earth splits and embraces her daughter.

Thus Sita, lives and dies at the same time as an ideal woman.

Sage Valmiki writes the story of Ramayana forever until he turns to an ant hill.

*   *   *

Next morning, we children played it out. Shovan, my little brother jumped from one end of the courtyard to the other acting out all the roles. One minute he was the coy Surpanakha with all her coquetry, the next minute he pretended to be the ferocious demon king, Ravan pulling Sita. I had such a belly laugh when he flung his thin limbs in the air pretending to be the strong bird Garur.

*   *   *

As I lifted up my face to grasp a breath I saw Jassimuddin, his face serious and stern. "Khukumoni, go get ready. Your mother is sick. Very sick. We must reach Mymensingh as soon as possible."

I did not understand the exact medical complication my mother had, but often she got very sick. Her face would turn pale and blue. She'd curl like a baby in fetal position, in pain.

We reached Mymensingh. The doctor came and gave her an injection and lots of medicine. I stood at the door—*Oh God don't take my Ma now, give her life, make her better. Please don't make her die.*

Then, I found that the doctor was staring at me. I took my eyes away. Next time I checked with a quick side glance, and he was still looking at me.

"This is not your child, is she?" he asked my parents.

"My daughter." My mother's voice was faint.

"Not *your real* daughter. I mean biological. Right?" This time he turned to my father.

"Well, no. Not in that sense. You know my wife could not have a child. So we adopted her. She is my wife's brother's child." My father confessed.

"Say that. Now it makes sense." The doctor smirked and slammed his little box with loud clicks.

"She looks more like her aunt from Bataspur, not like you or your wife."

Both our images reflected on the gigantic mirror on mother's dresser. For the first time I saw that it is true I looked more like my aunt, Baroma. I had nothing common with Ma or Baba. I am not theirs. I am a deserted child, a destitute girl, I am an orphan.

I ran to my room filled with uncontrollable sobs. Tried to reach for my special blanket, but felt it disgustingly fake. I threw my *nakshi kantha* across the room. My world shook. It became blank. Like nothing existed. Everything I knew felt like a big lie. I felt I was sinking. Sinking to a bottomless pit. People knocked on my door. I did not answer.

When the storm inside me stopped I took a deep breath and felt as if Padma was whispering—*I told you, if you betray, one of us will be hurt.*

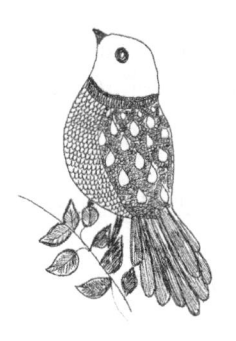

5
PALACE OF MUKTAGACHA

Ma came to my room all dressed up in her thousand dot *Dhakai* sari. She was looking exquisite today in that off white soft muslin. I heard that muslin was soft enough to pass through my father's wedding ring. And there were one thousand tiny gold dots on that six yards of sari, hand embroidered with golden thread. I gazed at her face. The chandelier earrings dazzled. She was beaming.

"You may wear something fancy too." She smiled and handed me the ivory color silk dress I loved so much and hardly found an occasion to wear. I jumped in joy.

"Really, this one!"

"Yes, we are going to the *Rajbari, palace of* Muktagachha. Now hurry up." She started tying a matching ivory satin bow braiding my hair. Opening the cherry wood armoire she took out her carved wooden jewelry box. A pair of wristlets shone on her palm.

"Mind you, these are heirloom jewelry, my mom's childhood bracelet. So be careful." Ma warned tying them on my wrists. The honey color stones shone with the most delicious translucent shades of melon, yellow and crimson. It felt I could even taste drops of honey in them. I kissed them.

"Now that's enough," Ma scowled.

"What are these stones called, Ma?"

"*Gomed*, a rare kind of garnet. They are potent, it is believed that it can takeaway the ill effect of the *Rahu*, on the person wearing it, if the wearer is going through a bad time."

"What is Rahu, Ma?

"That is an astrological thing. Khuku, you ask too many questions."

I skipped and bowed and smiled with a curtsy in front of the full length mirror.

"Khuku, listen. Listen very carefully, I don't want all these silliness. Such nonsenses are going to stay at home. I expect you to behave when you go there. We are going to a very special place today, to the palace of Muktagacha, and I don't want them to have any bad impression on you. You are past ten years old now. Many girls are even married at this age. Understand?"

"Yes. Ma."

"Tell me how are you going to show your best manners?"

"I will greet my elders with *pranam*, touching their feet and not interrupt when elders are talking."

"Good. You just be quiet. Listen, no talking unless asked a question. Because as soon you open your mouth you talk nonsense."

"Are there any children to play?" I asked.

"No, no children."

"Can I take my book?"

"No, there is no need to show off. You be modest, humble and obedient. And remember, you should not be greedy, because there may be lots of rich food. Can you handle that, if not, you may stay home." Ma was clear.

Dyspepsia and other stomach troubles went hand in hand with me those days. Ma tried to protect me from every possible thing allowing me only a very bland, horrible diet. Maybe it was good for my stomach but it was not good for my appetite, or for my spirit. I refused to eat anything she forced or even gave me with love. This robbed me of my normal nourishment. It was a terrible vicious circle.

I longed to eat delicious food. Tasty, savory, rich and sweet, even sour things like the pickles and chutneys with *kul (jujube fruit)*, green mango and tamarind. I had dreams of eating puffed fried loochis and wondered how monda really tasted. But my mother failed to understand that.

The opportunity to see the palace was a big thing in my boring uneventful life. I was looking forward to it. So I nodded politely.

"I'll remember, Ma."

Pochar ma, our maidservant showed off the grand display of the *sandesh* Ma was making this morning. It was a sweetmeat dish made with home made cheese and new molasses of the season. I could smell the sweet molasses from those cheese balls that were formed into tiny shapes of conches. Each of them perfectly molded. Pochar ma transferred them to an oval silver platter and covered with a crocheted doily.

"That's good." Ma approved, also Pochar ma's selection of the sari she wore for visiting the palace.

Chaitan and Noor, the two horses came out for this special occasion all decked up, in front of the portico. The carriage driver attached them with the carriage. We climbed the tonga and Jassim da sat with the driver.

Muktagacha was about ten miles west of Mymensingh, the driver announced.

The clip clop of the horses and the whirs of the wheels energized me. P*alash phools* blossomed with scarlet splashes against the blue sky. It reminded me that Holi, the festival of color was not far away. Spring was in the air.

Sweat glistened on the horses' bodies like drops of crystals as they picked up speed. A bulbul sang. S*ipahi bulbul*, Babu had shown me pictures of this special species in his 'Birds of India' book. I could see the little crown on the black bird and I made a mental note not to forget to tell him about this. He'd be excited.

Ma broke my chain of thought. She kept reminding me how I should remember my good manners by greeting the elders with *pranam,* bowing down and touching their feet; never to talk or intervene while grownups were talking unless I am asked a question, not to be greedy, et cetera.

When our carriage entered the estate and stopped in front of the royal palace of Muktagacha, my jaw dropped. I had never seen anything like this in my whole life, even in pictures. It gave me a shiver to think that I am related to this royal family, maybe a distant relative, maybe very distant one, but still!

I was awestruck by the beautiful marble statues. I wished to touch them and see if they were really so smooth. They were made of stone after all... how could something be so soft and so hard at the same time? The flowers around the fountain in the garden were almost unreal, as if someone had just painted them. I looked up. There were lattice and filigree designs on different parts of the building. Crystal lamps glistened from the chandeliers that hung from the ceilings.

Ma gave me a side glance with a blink, meaning I should check my posture. I got the point, straightened my shoulders, lifted my chin and walked like a ballerina as if I were quite used to seeing all these things.

Just then a tall, handsome man approached. He was wearing a long Nehru-coat with tight *churidar* pants. Ma whispered, "*Rajkumar,* the prince." Though the prince was strikingly handsome with sharp, dark features, he was not wearing any crown or jewelry. The prince came forward and bowed to Ma, "How are you, Boudi?" and smiled at me.

After exchanging greetings he called an assistant to take Ma and Pochar ma to the inside of the palace and asked if I would be interested in seeing the garden.

"Please, please!" I jumped in joy. "Please Ma." She gave me a look which meant remember what you promised about your manners. But she also nodded to the gentleman. As soon as Ma left I felt much at ease.

"So, you are my uncle, right? May I call you Uncle Prince?" I asked.

"Sure, I'll like that. but who told you that I am a prince?" he laughed.

"I know you are the prince, but where is your crown? I expected a crown on a prince."

"Maybe you can make me one. Then I'll wear it. So far no one has given me one. Now this is a very big estate, sprawling over ten acres of land. Where do you want to start?"

I gazed at the awesome palace and asked, "Is it true that once this palace was smashed into dust? What is the story?"

"You know that? Well, Maharaja Surjo Kanta built this palace first with the image of the Crystal Palace of London. It was all crystal and glass, each room a piece of art. That made many of his relatives very jealous. One day an elderly aunt could not hide it and remarked, 'Surjo, you did pour a lot of money, I can see. Why didn't you make it with silver instead of these fragile glasses and crystals?' It was just a comment, but in a short time there was a big earthquake. The infamous earthquake of 12th June 1897 and in that quake the whole palace crumpled into pieces."

"Tell me what happened to the palace then?" I went back.

"This new palace is built by his heir Sashikanta. Sashikanta made it stronger, earthquake proof and equally beautiful with crystals and glasses." He explained.

"My father told me that it is a mixture of Mughal architecture with Indo-European touch. He also told me that the zaminders of Muktagacha are connoisseurs of music, art and theater. And you even have a revolving stage. Is that true?"

"You are right. My, you know so much, I am quite impressed Khuku. I have never met a girl of your age interested in such things. We do have a revolving stage, one of the very first ones in Asia. It was broken during the earthquake but restored again. And we have hosted many dignitaries here like Rabindranath Tagore, the Duke of Russia, and many others. Are you interested to see our music room? But we will have to be very quiet since the musicians are probably practicing. I'd not dare to take just any child, but you are different."

"Yes please." I was excited. It felt great getting such compliments from an adult, especially from a prince.

SHADOW BIRDS

Through a winding path we meandered to another part of the garden. *Radhachura* blooms splashed vermillion blossoms on our path, and colored the blue sky above. He plucked a *jamrool* fruit from a bush and put one in my mouth and another in his own. We grinned at each other. Then we came to a beautiful pond and he helped me on a boat to a pretty gazebo in the middle of the pond. When I stood there it felt I was standing on the water, not on ground. It was a strange sensation. Then we went to visit the music room.

Uncle Prince brought me to the room where I met Ma. Pochar Ma was sitting on a low stool. As I entered the lady of the house hugged and kissed me on my forehead. I touched her feet showing my respect.

'You are becoming so pretty, but why so thin? We have to fatten you up." She smiled. I was hungry, very hungry by then and could smell something delicious in the air.

A young woman, older than me but much younger than Ma, entered the room with two platters in her hand. I was awestruck at her elegance, her ballerina like gait, the way her long braid swayed as she walked. She smiled at me and to show my respect I stooped to touch her feet. The lady jumped back, almost dropping the food.

"No. no, don't touch my feet!" She cried.

"What are you doing Khuku?" Ma scolded. Pochar ma started laughing exposing her ugly yellow big teeth.

The woman rested the bigger platter in front of Ma and the smaller in front of me. Ma, like an adroit eagle snatched the plate that was given to me. "Khuku will not be able to eat any of these. Her health does not allow such rich, good food." She gave back the platter with a fake smile.

Four tiny loochis, golden as the full moon, a serving of cauliflower fritters and a monda on a silver platter left me slowly, behind the lacy curtain.

I felt like screaming. I felt a lump in my throat, my eyes welled up. Ma did not notice it but the Lady of the House did.

She drew me closer and said, "Precious little one! I know what you will be able to eat." I loved the way she addressed me, 'precious one.' I'd always remember her. My Aunt of the Garden House, her plump, warm face lit with a big smile, filled with kindness remained in my heart.

"You are going to have the goat stew that was offered to the goddess."

That curry had a totally different taste. No onion, no garlic, or red pepper. It had a light taste of ginger, coriander, black pepper, cinnamon, bay leaf and a tinge of asafetida. I got well after eating that special stew.

*   *   *

When we came home Babu was resting on his recliner in their bedroom, sipping a cup of tea. Ma, in front of the oval mirror was undoing her hair, taking off the pins from her coiffeur. Babu asked,

"Had a good time?"

"Your daughter…!" Ma huffed taking off more pins.

"What did my daughter do?"

"Ah! She went and prostrated herself on the maid servant's feet!" Ma dramatized throwing her arm in the air.

"What can I say. And was she greedy! Seeing the food on the plate you wouldn't believe how your daughter drooled and finally started crying. Made me so embarrassed!" Ma swaying her cascading hair headed to take a shower.

Babu winked at me. "So you had a horrible, rotten day, hmm?"

I made sure that Ma was gone and the shower was on full swing; I came closer to my father and sat on the recliner handle.

"Actually I had a great day."

"Really? Tell me, tell me."

I told him about the Prince, the gazebo in the lake, the revolving stage and the music room where I had seen *sarod, beena* and sitar. These musical instruments, except the sitar, were all new to me. I managed sitting quietly for a long time while the musicians were practicing and as a reward they let me touch and play those instruments.

I told him about Prince Charming and how he was so humble and down to earth.

Then I told him about the very attractive lady who was just a maid servant and I mistakenly took her as one of our relatives. She was not at all like Pochar ma.

I shared with my father the story of the *hookah* hierarchy that I had experienced in the village a while ago.

"I wonder what is class, Babu? Is putting down people, making them aware over and over that they are not as good as us called class? Is that what aristocrat people do?"

Babu smiled. "You had a long, interesting day, my child. Now go sleep."

"Babu, I forgot to tell you something. I spotted a Sipahi Bulbul today. It does have a crown indeed. A crown of a king or a soldier? Sipahi means soldier, doesn't it?"

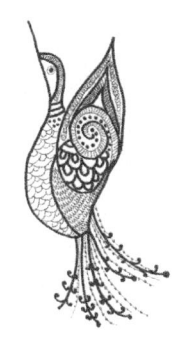

6

PIYARI, THE ELEPHANT

I remember the elephants. There were one hundred elephants in the Muktagacha palace. On the *Bijoya Dashami* day, when the clay image of the goddess Durga had to be immersed in the river, all the elephants came out.

Bajra Prasad led the procession, adorned with a silver-plated *hawdah* on his back with velvet cushion seats and glittery sequins hanging from them. He accompanied his fiancee, Rabi. Rabi had elaborate designs drawn on her entire trunk, and her two eyebrows were painted with vermillion dust and sandalwood paste. The other elephants ambled behind them protecting the float of the image of Mother Durga. In between, jugglers showed off their tricks, dancers pranced with fire and incense sticks in their hands and the *dhakis* drummed their enormous drums.

Arms and ammunition were displayed. On the veranda, in front of the temple, guns and knives, arrows and bows were brought and laid in order, about thirty or forty of them. They were cleaned, polished and finally decorated with sandalwood paste designs. We prayed for the arms to be blessed.

We, the children, sat in a circle with wild amazement listening to our elders telling the stories and history of each weapon. "This rifle was used to kill the horrible man-eater Royal Bengal tiger that had eaten up eleven villagers in such and such year," or "Do you know which one Uncle Manu used for the elephant that went crazy, breaking its enclosure trap and all the metal bars?" Then one of them would add, "Do you know the story of the lost tiger that came to visit from the Garo Hills?" We children shouted out, "Please tell us."

"Well, once a tiger decided to come down the Garo hills and take a tour of the valley. Ten or twelve miles south of Netrokona city rumors began that people have seen a ferocious tiger.

It was a huge tiger with black stripes on its ochre yellow body. Every now and then villagers were missing cows and goats. Now the tiger was stuck and scared too. It did not expect that there would be so much hustle bustle in the towns and bazaars. So what could it do? It hid itself in the vinery of betels and settled there temporarily, but how long could this go on? After sun-down it came out in search of food but now the people around were aware and started making noises. The tiger was very disturbed.

Among the zaminder clan there were quite a few who were passionate about hunting, especially for a lonely, lost tiger. Each wanted to show his talent in this sport. They came out with swinging guns on their shoulders.

All day long they wandered and wandered and then reported how they had heard the sound of the tiger relishing the bones and meat of its prey. But what could these hunters do? They had to proceed with great caution. If you failed and the tiger won, it would taste the blood of a human and then it would turn into a man-eater. Who would rescue the poor villagers then? Therefore, the hunters decided to return home. Luckily, the tiger also found its way back to the hills and that is the end of this story."

We children had a big sigh of relief and clapped wildly.

*   *   *

I'll never forget Piyari Chanchal. He was an adolescent elephant like me, same age, or maybe a bit older. Like an active, restless little boy, he loved to play in the water and would not come out. He would thump and clomp and play in the muddy pool, spray and splash with his trunk. He was very fond of my second cousin, Kutti dada.

No one could get him out of the water even when it got dark. "Get up elephant, it is time to go home," the *mahut* (elephant keeper) shouted, but Piyari Chanchal would not listen, until Kutti dada bribed him with bananas and coconuts and cajoled him, stroking his trunk, "Chanchal *shona*, my love, I promise you another day to play again." The elephant swayed his trunk and listened to him but not to grownups at all.

Elephants and people have a lot in common. Their life spans are similar to ours. I heard that in their late sixties and seventies they get the same health problems that humans face. They suffer from heart troubles, arthritis, shortness of breath, just like us.

When they are little, they depend on their moms solely like we do. The elephant mom teaches them how to use the trunk for eating, cleaning, drinking and also how to greet. Like we learn to use our hands. When they are thirteen or so, they enter puberty like we do and soon become adults. Around twenty they are able to have babies.

Piyari Chanchal also had one of those crazy days of puberty. One day he took us, a bunch of people to the river side on his back. The sun was going down in the Brahmaputra River. The western sky blushed with vermilion and lustful pink. Piyari Chanchal had seen it all.

After he reached the portico, he gently sat, folding his rear legs to let each one of us get down. Then he rushed, shook the *mahut* off and started to run. The *mahut* was a bit perplexed in the beginning, then he grinned "*Zara masti aye*" *(*got a bit high), he remarked.

Piyari Chanchal started running around, banging the iron gate, messing up the stalls in the market. When some tried to prevent him, he turned them upside down. He attacked the cars and the horses on the main road. People got hurt and many shops lost their merchandise.

He was marked as a mad elephant. The District Magistrate ordered, "Shoot the damn elephant." Probably the Magistrate was encouraged by George Orwell's books and wanted to be a hero for shooting an elephant. Now, the Magistrate did not have any tools to do the job, so he asked the zaminder.

The sandalwood adorned rifle was taken down from the wall and handed over to the boss. What could he do? You may be a Raja of some place, but when an order came from the British headquarters, you had to obey.

Piyari Chanchal was a beloved elephant of our extended family. Kutti da's grandfather, could not accept his murder. Every now and then the sound of that bullet echoed in his brain. For the next few days he kept himself isolated in a dark room, not eating, not doing anything. It was a strange mourning session he dedicated for the elephant. Kutti da was in college in Calcutta. So luckily he did not have to experience it.

I thought of Piyari Chanchal a lot. Felt that such bouts of exhilaration did come to me too sometimes. There were times when I wished if I could just run run run up the Garo hills, through the green rice fields, swim in the Brahmaputra River, dive and sink like a fish, hug someone tight and kiss…

Piyari Chanchal, by nature was much active, more energetic. But he was a teenager like me after all. Maybe he did it a bit too much but for that should he be killed? And we had no voice to protest it?

I flung my school bag on the floor. My throat felt dry, my mouth, bitter. I wished I could cry. Only a black void, a sadness as big as that dear elephant kept swirling in my chest and crept up to burst inside my brain.

Ma entered the room. "Look at you, your face looks like a dry mango. What happened?"—She touched my forehead. "No you don't have a fever."

"Do you know that Piyari Chanchal has been killed?" my voice choked.

"Of course I do. What are you going to do with a mad elephant?"

I jerked and brushed her hand away and thumped my feet in anger leaving the room.

"Oh my! What a tantrum. Who are you showing all that temper to, hmm? You need to grow up girl, You must learn grace and humility and how to be nice. At your age I was already married. How will you handle it when you are married and live with your in-laws?"

I stormed to my room and slammed the door. This was my first experience with death. Death of a loved one. Maybe he was not a human, but I loved him. We played, he took me riding on his back, I painted on his back, fed him, cajoled him, he caressed me with his trunk, we were friends. We loved each other.

I felt like screaming, hiding my face under a pillow, and wanting to have a good cry. But that did not happen. I remained motionless with all that suffering stuffed up, alone. At one time I got up and started revolving around myself like a rotating firework until I felt dizzy. In the mirror many images of me kept on whirling like those Sufi monks who meditate like that, arms stretched out revolving and dancing at their own center. I looked like those meditating monks.

Then I was tired and plopped onto my bed. The chess board on a table across the room came into my vision, swirling ferociously. When it stopped I narrowed my eyes and to my amazement found that they were not just chess figurines any more. They were alive. They had lives.

From Babu's library I could hear music. Dara-ra-ra, dara-ra-ra… dara-ra-ra-ra-ra-ra-rung! Beethoven's fifth symphony. I felt goosebumps.

On the chess board the black soldiers, the horses, the bishops and the queen stepped one by one and in groups with the beat of the music and captured the white king's castle. The king was totally stuck. All the white soldiers, his horses, bishops, rooks, even the white queen were rolling on the board now. Lifeless. The black soldiers were glistening in sweat and blood with their swords and shields adorned in sandalwood paste blessed by the goddess. They were demanding from the white king, "Why this injustice?"

The music in the other room was in crescendo to celebrate. *Don't you worry Piyari Chanchal dear, one day we'll straighten it out.*

7
BABU

My father and my mother were very different in nature. They had very different approaches in rearing me. Ma was strict and stern. She made sure that I got the right message regarding manners, and that I follow through. She did not care if in the process, I got hurt.

Babu, on the other hand, had a more lenient, permissive way. I was free to ask anything and everything to him, no matter how silly or stupid it may be. When he did not know the answer he did not hesitate to say, "I don't know." I came to learn that even grownups did not know everything and that was okay and there was no shame in admitting it.

Many times, after days or weeks, he'd come back with the answer, show it in a book or explain it. I understood that he cared and valued my curiosity.

One day I asked him, "Babu, how are babies born?" He kept scratching his bald head, unsure how to answer that to a nine-year-old child. A couple of months later one day he called me and hurried me to the barn. I saw how a calf was born, coming out of its mother's body.

Babu was very different in nature from that of my mother's side of the aristocratic zaminders. He looked different too. He did not have their smooth fair complexion, or the round, plump physique. He was tall and lanky, with antique copper tanned skin. He was a head taller than most men I knew and walked with a hunched gait.

Babu did not have the happy-go-lucky contentment of the zaminders either. There was always a certain sadness in his eyes behind the glasses.

I had overheard that he was from a poor class. His father was a schoolmaster. My Babu was poor but smart. He was well read, intellectual, had a Master's degree in Liberal Arts and my grandfather chose him as his son-in-law because of those attributes.

He'd be an asset to the family for deciphering legal documents, reading, understanding them thoroughly. That way they'd be able to take action judiciously- my grandfather thought, and embraced Babu as his son in law. Grandfather stationed him in the city instead of the remote village of Batashpur and gave him the job to collect taxes, record them and do all the official business.

But my father failed. He felt stuck when the poor farmers fell to his feet and cried, telling him the stories of a death in the family or other catastrophes. He could not help remembering his own childhood days, the death of his own mother when he was a child.

I saw that his eyes would get sad and sadder and when the farmers begged to have their tax waived, he could not be strict or strong. The farmers kissed his feet with "God bless you. You are kind. God bless you!" But that gave Babu no comfort. His job was to collect money from them. He'd feel frustrated, inefficient, good-for-nothing and he sat in the darkness all alone looking at the stars.

In a few days rumors would creep and come to him through the grapevine. Waves of criticism and judgement would float in the form of gossip.

This is when he found a friend, Dr. Kader Choudhury, my best friend Padma's dad.

I called Dr. Kader, uncle Kader. He understood the void in Babu.

Their friendship provided the mutual nourishment that their intellectual souls craved. One day Babu announced that the zaminder of Kalikapur, Mr. Abani Kanta had made a Battery Room, meaning he had bought a generator where electricity could be created. People would be able to listen to the radio now. The idea of a transistor radio was still far away.

This was an era when hand drawn fans were in fashion among the affluent. *Pankhawala,* servants would pull huge cords of long cloth that provided cool air. This way the rich people cooled their rooms on hot muggy summer afternoons. Now an electric fan whirred in that room and a radio brought voices from far away.

"Want to go check out Netaji's speech tomorrow, Doc?" Babu's eyes twinkled. Netaji Subhas Chandra Bose had a different idea of bringing freedom to India (very different from Gandhi), ousting the British Raj, and people were interested to hear him.

The room was full. Common villagers and students from cities and towns gathered, spilling onto the adjoining veranda. In this whole area there was only one radio. Some people poked their heads through the window to see, but there was nothing to see, just to hear.

Inside, the zaminder clan relaxed stretching their bodies on the divans with throw pillows. They played chess and *pasha* with money while the servants brought tea on trays. This was something new. People were not used to drinking tea until recently, the tea boards of Assam introduced it one day in the village market fair in Gouripur and distributed it free. From then on some of them got hooked and some embraced the culture of serving tea to their guests. But we children were not allowed until we were old enough. I saw Babu and Uncle Kader were enjoying drinking the tea and listening to the radio.

But it was not Bengali. It was not Netaji's voice either. "Hitler. Adolf Hitler. Hitler is giving a speech in German," Dr. Kader cried out. He had been to Germany one time as a medical student, so he was the only one who understood what was going on. The rest of the mob listened to it with wild amazement, not understanding a single word but excited anyway.

*   *   *

On our way back, the covers of the phaeton were taken off. The breeze on my cheek and in my hair was cool and soothing.

Golden stalks on the new harvest swayed back and forth with waves of ochre under the blue sky. A ribbon of green adorned a distant field.

"Do you know we are going to have a terrible famine soon, an epidemic rushing to our door?" my father blurted.

What? There is so much abundance around, right here in Mymensingh... the earth is filled with crops. What is he talking about?

Many years later, after several decades maybe, I came to know about this horrible artificial famine of 1943, the infamous Bengal Famine, a manmade holocaust which was created by profit maximizing hoarders and the ruling class. Three million people died of malnutrition, hunger and disease, while nature was bountiful.

Babu recited:
> *Sweet is the lore which Nature brings,*
> *Our meddling intellect*
> *Mis-shapes the beauteous form of things*
> *We murder to dissect.*

"Okay Mr. Wordsworth." Dr. Kader smiled. Babu took a deep breath.

"It's no time for joke, Doc. I have heard that it has approached Dhaka, Faridpur, Noakhali. There is no food. Common people are begging in the streets for just a bowl of *phan-* (the starch water that you drain off after cooking rice). It's pathetic. Cholera broke out. And how far are these places? Just a hundred miles or even less?

Really it's not a joke Doc. A guy from Gouripur, the other day started yelling in the marketplace that the price of jute has gone up four fold in a month and will be up more. Jute is our main crop. This guy, half crazy you may say, hollered—Mark my words, I am Muhammad Nooro, I roam around the office bureau." Dr. Kader laughed at that rhyming, and Babu joined in.

Then they became serious. Babu and Uncle Kader started talking about things serious like feudalism, imperialism and anarchism. Nice tongue twisters as I practiced them whispering to myself. But what do they mean? They were talking about things that were going over my head and I was feeling bored until I heard,

"Well, Bhabani babu, don't you forget that you are not one of those common people. You are not part of the poor farmers or fishermen, you are not the proletariat class. You are a bourgeois from the aristocratic, bureaucratic class whose interest is against that of the common people. Actually your class exploits the common people, no matter how empathetic you pretend to be. Whatever class consciousness you may have, you are not one of them."

Babu's face went purple and then pale, as if someone had just slapped him on the cheek. Silence. Absolute silence. No one talked for a while. Only the whirs of the wheels went on and on.

*   *   *

"Well, we have all heard stories of treacheries and oppressions done by the selfish zaminder. Here is the tale of a helpless sad one," Dr. Kader broke the silence.

"Once upon a time there lived a Hindu zaminder named Indra Kanta. Indra Kanta was the zaminder of a place called Kagamari. His boss was the Nawab of Murshidabad, It was the Mughal era, two hundred years from now, before the British took over. Murshid Kuli Khan of Murshidabad ruled this area. When Indra could not collect all the taxes from his people and failed to pay his share, the Nawab punished him. Tortured him to the extreme, to the extent that the Hindu zaminder had to sacrifice his religion. 'If you cannot pay me the money, give me your faith, commanded the Nawab.' Indra Kanta was forced to become Muslim. His name and identity were changed to Inayatullah Choudhury. Can you imagine the shame, the insult and torture he went through?"

Babu said, "Of course. I have heard another story like this. It was about the Maharaja of Sushong. When Rana Singh, the king of Sushong died, his two young boys were commanded to pay the taxes. They were still not adults. The children had just lost their dad and had no clue what levies, and taxes meant. It was decided that because of this failure the oldest prince would be whipped naked in front of his subject, That would teach him what rights and responsibilities were all about.

An old servant appeared and thrust himself forward covering the young prince. Bancharam was his name. 'Please do not touch the royal body. It is not his fault that the payment could not be made in time. Lash me if you need to, do not touch our prince. We promise to pay you soon', said this loyal servant. The prince was spared." Babu sighed.

"Uncle Kader, are you one of the heirs of that Inayatullah, Indra Kanta?"—the words darted out of my mouth. I felt so embarrassed. I wished I could take them back. I bit my tongue. I wished to slap my own face. *Why do I do such silly things? This is why Ma warns me not to meddle in adults' conversation. Now what do I do?*

Uncle Kader stared at my face for a little while, then lowered his head smiling. Babu nodded with a chuckle. No one said anything more.

8

SWEET DELICACY

"Did you eat the Monda here, Khukumoni?" Uncle Kader asked me.

"Monda? I have never tasted a monda in my life. Never ever, anywhere." I pouted.

"You are kidding. That is the specialty of Muktagacha, our pride, and you never ate a monda yet?" Then he looked at Babu and said "How about we stop for some tea?"

"Muktagacha is on the other side, at least ten miles due west, isn't it?" Babu answered.

"Yes, brother, but before that, there is another place, much closer, who makes equally good monda and there is a story. I'll treat Miss Khukumoni today with this sweet delicacy, something that she'll never forget in her whole life, never, ever." He grinned.

I was relieved that Uncle Kader did not take offense at my silly curiosity or was generous enough to forgive me for that.

*   *   *

A slight turn from the Kestopur Main road brought us in front of a big pond, almost a lake. Right in front of it stood a shack which turned out to be a tiny shop made of bamboo poles and cheap jute. If you looked closely, you'd see a lopsided tin sign swinging in the air. It read Mahim's Monda. The shop was empty. Different kinds of sweets were displayed in the glass case, but the inside was dark and muggy. Uncle Kader instructed the *tonga* driver to take the horses to the lake for a drink and to cool off.

Babu strolled towards the waterfront reciting in his tenor voice, "The world is busy finding success in strength and power. I made my home here in this village of Bengal. I have seen the face of Bengal, I need not search for beauty of this earth any where, any more."

"Jibanananda Das. From *Rupashi Bangla* (The Beautiful Bengal)," appreciated Uncle Kader.

"I like this modern poet a lot. He brings a distinct new flavor, doesn't he?" Babu remarked.

"Look here, Babu, is this the monda shop, you were talking about?" I cried out.

"Yes, and it has a story. Did you ever hear the name Gopal Pal? Does it ring a bell?" Dr. Kader looked at Babu.

"Famous for his special monda. Wasn't he?"

"Yes. Almost a hundred years ago, around 1824-25 this Gopal Pal won the heart of the queen of Muktagacha with his special sweet. So much so that the queen hired him as the royal chef. Since then his heirs are still making mondas in the royal kitchen of Muktagacha. Other sons and their sons are opening up businesses around the town using this ancestral credential. One thing they never release is the recipe of this sweet dish. A top secret. It must remain in the family. Utmost confidential." Dr. Kader put a finger to his lips.

"That is why you'd never find mondas anywhere else other than Muktagacha. You see, you may get Natore's famous *kachagolla*, or Dhaka's specialty dessert *bakorkhani* even if you go to Kolkata, but not the mondas." His eyes were big and round as he looked at me. Then he started again:

"Once upon a time this Mahim Musselman was not Muslim but a Hindu potter. His name was Aswini Kumar Pal. They were clay artists by trade. They made statues of gods and goddesses. Aswini's father fancied naming his offspring after the celestial stars. Aswini's brother was Bharani, his two sisters, Krittika and Rohini."

"I know those stars Krittika, Rohini, Mrigoshira, Adra," I burst out.

"Okay, okay, don't have to show off so much, Khuku. Go on with your story, Doc." Babu said picking up a pebble from the path as we approached the shop.

Doctor Kader continued, "Well, one summer the dad fell ill. Got smallpox. Within a week he was gone. Not only that, he took along his wife, Aswini's mother and the little brother, Bharani.

After cremating them when Aswini came back home he faced the burden that was left for him. Life. For the first time, he realized that now he was in charge of running the household, managing the financial debt of his father that crept up to his chest and the responsibility of marrying off his two sisters. Where would he get all that money? He settled a wedding for Krittika, his sister, with an old, old man from his clan with a large dowry. The groom died within a year and Krittika came back as a boomerang." He took a break. Then started, "Aswini went to the sons of Gopal Pal; they were distantly related. Hearing his sad story the Pals agreed to hire him as a helper in one of their shops. Within a short time, Aswini made his way to the kitchen from being dishwasher boy. Aswini was smart. He learned the trick, the recipe of making the mondas." Uncle Kader paused as someone came to greet us.

A person with a small stature, a tiny face with pointy ears and a shaved head appeared and stood in front of us with a wide smile. He greeted the doctor folding his hands and bringing them to his chest "Namaskar". Then immediately he clicked his bare feet together and saluted in a military way. Then he nodded his head and stuck out his little tongue, as if he was embarrassed, and gave a salam uttering *"Selam Alliakum."*

The doctor could not help laughing, "Alliakum Selam, Rebati. How are you? Are you taking your medicine regularly?"

The little man poked out his tongue again, licked his lips and started scratching his bare head. "N-n-n-o more m-m-edicine left. Get af-af-after Puja. N-n-no money now." He was relieved to finish the sentence.

"Rebati, that's no excuse. You must take the medicine every day. I told you. Pay later, don't pay, I don't care, but you need them every day."

"M-m-mother said n-n-no pay doctor, n-n-o healing," he nodded his head.

"I see. Tell your mother what I said. Pay me later, when you can what you can, even it does not matter to me if you can't."

"M-m-ma dead. I call Mahim," he hurried to run inside.

Then he came back again and started getting busy moving the furniture inside and brought the table outside all by himself. "C-c-cooler outside" he explained.

Babu helped him with the wooden benches and we set a nice picnic style under the shade of the big banyan tree in front of the shop. Rebati set up another spot with tables and chairs under another shady tree nearby for the next guests.

Right then moving the jute curtain another man appeared. He looked a little older, in his mid-forties maybe, kind of a plump fellow with very dark skin. On his bare ebony body, sweat glistened, especially on his protruding round belly. He quickly wiped off the sweat from his forehead and arms with a red and white typical *gamcha*, put on a green *fotua* shirt and grinned.

"What a pleasant surprise, doctor. After such a long time! Tell us what may I offer you. Made some fresh cutlets, came out right now." Then he touched his two earlobes with his two hands, sticking out his tongue (a gesture saying, sorry, forgive me) and said "I do notice now the sacred thread on this Brahmin guest of yours." He pointed to Babu. "That cutlet is of beef, can't offer that to him. But sirs, we have some cauliflower samosas freshly prepared, how about that with some nice *cha*?"

Dr. Kader nodded. "Sounds good. Mahim, what about your special *monda*? I told them about your *monda*, and how you learned the secret recipe of this special sweet. Why don't you tell us that story yourself?"

"Of course, sir. We have fresh *mondas* too. Prepared early this morning. And for *Chordimoni* (little sister addressed in an affectionate way) I'll bring some freshly steamed milk." Mahim gave me a smile and disappeared behind the curtain.

Dr. Kader picked up the thread of his story, "How far did I tell? Where was I?"

"That Mahim learned the secret recipe and the trick to make the monda" I replied. Dr. Kader rolled his eyes and chuckled. "Look at this curious listener!"

"Well. Aswini's little sister, Rohini, remember her? She is now a budding woman of seventeen." He paused. Dr. Kader hunted his pockets to take out the cigarette box. In a slow motion, he took one cigarette out of the box, struck it three times on the wooden table, then offered one to Babu. Babu took out a matchbox from his *kurta* pocket, then lit it and both shared the flame. Dr. Kader took a long inhale and made circles of smoke, rolling his tongue.

I felt very jittery. My toes started tapping the ground. *Come on, what happened then?* But I knew better. It is not polite to show such impatience. I just had to wait.

"Yes, in front of their house was a big pond. One side was used by the Hindu neighborhood, the other side, by the Muslim folks who lived there. While Rohini went to fetch water, with the brass *kalsi* tucked at her side hip, she met a Muslim chap from the other side. Then you know what happens, right?" With a little pause, he added, "They got attracted to each other and fell in love. Hossain wanted Rohini, Rohini wanted Hossain." Uncle Kader took a break to shake off the ashes from his cigarette. Mahim entered with plates full of samosas, mondas and teas.

"Here is the fresh steamed milk from our own cow, little sister. Tell me how you like my monda." He put a plate in front of me.

Dr. Kader invited him. "Oh Mahim, come sit with us. Tell us your story about Rohini and Hossain." He scooted to make room for Mahim on the wooden bench.

"What can I say Sir? When I learned what my sister had done, what they were up to I felt like I should strike a hard bamboo pole on her head and throw her in the well!" Mahim's eyes flared, his voice shrilled. I shivered to see such ferocious feature in this sweet man who appeared to be quite calm and gentle just a minute ago. Then he took a breath, calmed himself and in his special dialect began:

"Then Sir, Hossains brother Rahmat came to me one day and told me—'Aswini, look, we want to take your sister among us with love, with dignity. You don't have to pay a single *paisa* dowry, rather if you ever need to start something on your own, a business or open a shop, Hossain may help you, financially. He has a good job and earns good money. He will be able to take care of your sister very well. They are a good match.' Rahmat said, 'Aswini, what did your Hindu religion give you? You are a potter now, you will be a potter always, the same low caste. The Brahmins will not eat with you, you will not be able to enter wherever you want to. You won't be accepted.

In our Muslim religion, we are all brothers. There is no such caste distinction, such superiority complex. Besides, where do you have the money to wed your sisters in your clan? Think about it. Give up your Hindu religion. Join us. Let your sister be happy.'

It was a serious decision, sirs. What he had told me was true. Hundred percent true. So I decided to change. I let go. I became a Muslim. From Aswini Kumar Pal I became Mahim Musselman." Aswini paused, ran his tongue over his lips and continued.

"Next day when I went back to my work, oh the way they treated me! As if I was not to be touched. They did not let me enter the kitchen. No one would drink water if I fetched it. They only allowed me to be a dishwasher all day long, even not to serve the tables. I felt so insulted that I quit. Then they accused me of stealing from the cash box! Is this the way to treat people? Your own cousin? Just because I became poor, just because I had to change my religion, and become a Muslim, you treat me like dirt?

It was Hossain who saved me. Like a real brother he stretched his hand to pick me up when I had fallen. 'Take my money now, brother and stand on your feet. I trust that you'll make it,' he said. That gave me the strength to open this store. It is going fine, sirs. *Inshallah! Mash Allah!*" He thanked someone up in the sky.

"He was right. Within a year I paid back all that I had borrowed, all that I owed. Now I am free. Now I make good money. I work hard, people like it. People are good. Life is better. *Mash Allah!*" Then he smiled at me, "*Chordimoni*, how was the *monda*?"

"Very nice." I smiled back. I tasted nothing like this before. This round, soft, sweet thing was creamy like a ball of yogurt, not quite, and then crunchy on the top. So different from all the sweetmeats I had tasted ever before and very delicious indeed. Really it is a Mymensingh delicacy, absolutely unique.

* * *

Mahim started again pointing to the funny person "Now look at this fellow, our Rebati. He is my cousin, my uncle's son, but he was raised by my father. Rebati had lost his parents when he was very small. My father named him after the star Rebati.

"Rebati is the last, the twenty-eighth wife of the Moon," I blurted.

"Something like that, my father might have known, not me. Rebati considered my father as his own dad. He comes, helps me out, lives with us maintaining all his Hindu rituals and then leaves suddenly. Who knows where he goes! Does not talk much. Then he appears all of a sudden. He has to come back here. Come for the milk at least. You know he has a little addiction to opium and opium addicts do need milk. So he comes. But one thing doctor, Rebati will never give up his religion. No one can take it away from him. That I know for sure. He plays the *dhaak* in front of the goddess Ma Durga and that is his livelihood. You know what this rascal says? 'I can't leave my Ma. She never left me,' big philosopher, eh?" Mahim nodded his head and concluded, "I don't know what that means doctor, but I know that no one can take his faith away from this boy."

*   *   *

A group of people arrived. They were laughing. "Hey, Mahim, smells good cutlet frying. May we have some cha too?" one of them hollered.

"Sure! Whatever you wish, your majesty." Mahim laughed too. Mahim introduced them to us.

"This is Hossain, my brother-in-law and his big brother, Rahmat, my friend, and this is our leader, Aziz Ahmed. He is the best *lathial (stick master)* around here. We are all scared of him because he can do anything if he wants to." Mahim winked and patted him on the shoulder.

"And this is Doctor Kader Choudhury. There are very few people on earth as generous and kind like him. He is a superb doctor too. The best doctor. Anything happens we all go to him. And this is Bhabani babu, Dr. Kader's dear friend and his daughter."

Hossain and Rahmat nodded to us and greeted, "Selam Alliakum" gesturing with their hands, touching their foreheads.

The man named Aziz came forward. He was taller than Babu, six feet or even more, very well built, wearing a *pathloon (cotton long pants)* and a *sando genji* (wife-beater sleeveless shirt) showing off his muscles. He turned to Dr. Kader.

"Doctor, you are aware of our team, the branch of Muslim League in Mymensingh, aren't you? We have invited you, but you never came to our meetings. We need people like you." He said that to Dr. Kader totally ignoring Babu and me.

"I am a doctor, you see. I don't have much time left after seeing my patients. Besides." Dr. Kader replied.

"Besides what? Besides what doctor?" He narrowed his eyes,

marching another step closer to the doctor. Dr. Kader scooted back.

"Never mind. It's getting late. I have to check on a patient." Dr. Kader checked his pocket watch.

We were getting ready to go home. The driver helped me climb into the phaeton. As I looked up, I saw that this Aziz man was staring at me. It was a strange stare, a nasty one. I had never experienced anything like that before. It chilled me and shook me inside at the same time, as if someone stripped me naked.

All the way home a creepy feeling terrified me and I could not get it out of my mind. I felt nauseated. Then when I reached home, I threw up. Threw up all that sweet delicacy.

9

THE DANCER'S PRAYER

Pardon me o Lord
I am just a dancer.
May my gesture express my homage
Through music.

My heart trembles in pain
Ripples bob in the ocean of peace
I pray-
May my dedication not die
Before it reaches your feet.
I bring no flower,
Nor fruit,
Nor a vessel of holy water.

I bring me,
My energy
As an offering to thee.

"We will do a show. We will do a show!" Padma, my friend, clapped her hands, jumping in joy. "*Pujarini*, the dance drama, for our annual show, Soi!," her eyes twinkled. She held me in a tight embrace.

Before I could understand anything I heard the loudspeaker announcing that all senior girls are supposed to meet at the school's front yard.

Our teachers stated that for the annual program this year, the students of the senior-most class may put up a dance drama and the piece that had been selected is *Pujarini*.
"Now, girls, we want to know what do you know about this piece. What do you understand?"

A tiny girl with thick glasses and a serious face raised her thin hand and in a shrill, high-pitched voice demonstrated a thorough command over the subject. She impressed us. We never knew this unassuming character before.

Pujarini, the Devotee, is a poem by Rabindranath Tagore which he penned later in a dance drama form, as *Notir Puja* -The Dancer's Prayer. The story is about a court-dancer which is based on a Buddhist legend.

King Ajatsatru (491 BC—461 BC) was against Buddhism. He ordered that anyone attempting the spread of Buddhism in his kingdom, either in the form of prayers, worship or any other demonstration, will be executed.

Srimati, a simple court dancer, steadfast in her devotion to Lord Buddha, with a platter filled with offerings of flowers and fruits moves on to show her homage. The King's mother sees her. Shocked at the girl's foolishness, she stops her, reprimands her and reminds her of the royal decree.
Srimati, a smile in her face, chin held high, strolls along towards the temple. The King's wife trembles at her audacity. Scolds her that she might be banished or even killed. Didn't she hear the King's prohibition?

Srimati, nonchalant, glides, swaying her long braided tassel. Her anklets jingle as she approaches the window of Princess Shukla who was reading a book at that leisurely afternoon. The book drops. Princess Shukla, awestruck at the firm rebel of this common dancer, screams, 'Go back, foolish girl! Hide, before anyone sees you like this!'

The dancer wanders in her steady, confident gait to reach the altar, *stupa*. She bestows her offering to the Lord Buddha. Then she dances. The royal command glistens on the silver sword slashing the praying girl's head.

Our teachers were happy with our basic knowledge. Now it is time for a demonstration.

"You are the topmost class of the school. The senior class. Through your demonstration of this drama, you are going to show your understanding of the subject matter. This will include history, geography, language, art—all the faculties. It's your chance to research these things thoroughly and we'll guide you as teachers, give you resources—but it is your journey, your show in teamwork. Clear?"

Bokuldi, our teacher, energized us. For the next few months we researched the architecture of the buildings and palaces of that era to design the backdrops of the stage. We studied what people wore in those days to design the costumes. Huge patterns were created on transparent papers and sewing machines whirred.

In the music department, the girls practiced in chorus to get the songs right. But the best was the dance.

I watched Ashmani dance. She was portraying Srimati. Her slender body swayed like a weeping willow as if each part had something to say. She shimmied in joy, broke herself from the waist swaying, showing agony, twirled and pranced to paint her ecstasy, stretching her arms wide like an albatross. Then she folded and gathered them to her bosom gesturing how her heart could blossom like a flower.

SHADOW BIRDS

She skipped and gyrated in wide circles to show her confidence on the dance floor. Her footwork, quick tapping with the beats of the *tabla* spoke of her steadfastness, and then she brought herself to a complete stop at the precise beat, at a crescendo. The whole thing was a dancer's prayer indeed.

Ashmani was trained in *Kathak* dance and she was a talented artist. The combination came out alive in the choreography.

I wished I could dance like that. But I had no such training, no such talent. At the end of the day, after I came back home, I fancied dancing like her, being aware of each part of my body, making it as beautiful as it could be. Speak with my body.

The afternoon sun cast a long shadow on the ground. I started dancing with my shadow.

Then, one day Padma sneaked into the courtyard. I did not notice that. Then she clapped, "Encore, encore. Not bad. Not bad at all."

* * *

A new problem cropped up at school. The recital was supposed to be held on the Saraswati Puja day. Saraswati Puja is a major festival for all Hindu students. Every Hindu school observes this and looks forward to it with fond anticipation.

Saraswati is the goddess of learning, art, and music. She is the muse for artists and writers. We visualize her in her snow-white form, gliding from the heaven, down through the Himalayas, riding on a swan, with a lyre in her hand. She would come and rest on the big lotus flower we have arranged for her, to bless us.

Now we came to know that some Muslim families raised opposition participating in the event. It is against their faith to observe idol-worshipping. They did not want their children to be part of it.

The school committee was in trouble. Though there were many Muslim students, Christian and Buddhists, the school was basically a Hindu school. It was founded by a Hindu zaminder, the Maharaja of Muktagacha. To commemorate the love for his mother, he named the school after his mother. Major financial donations came from his house. So there was no question that the recital as an extension of the Saraswati Puja celebration will not be cancelled. They did not want to force anyone against their religious faith, either.

The school committee solved it by issuing a new rule. Every participating student must bring their guardian's approval signature.

*   *   *

At home, I had another set of problems. We had guests. Everybody was busy with them. My grandfather had come from a long pilgrimage tour and stopped to pay us a visit on his way back home.

He was a widower and unlike most widower men of his time who remarried right after their wives died he spent his life like a Hindu widow, single, eating only a vegetarian diet, and wearing white clothes. He spent the last part of his life in a spiritual quest and pilgrimage.

A whole bunch of widowed ladies followed him, especially on these pilgrimage tours. Who would otherwise take them or what would happen to their afterlives—was their logic. They believed that visiting certain temples, traveling to holy places will make them pious, add good karma, especially to their afterlives.

We had not only one grandfather guest but five other women, which kept us occupied, especially my mother.

One day I told Ma about the guardian's approval thing in school asking for her signature.

"Just forget it. In our family girls do not go dancing in public. It is considered cheap. We do not do that. Now your grandfather is here. What kind of impression would he get, you think?" she brushed me away.

It shocked me. I could go to my father but he had been sick for a while. I had never seen Babu this sick, this weak. He had no appetite and every evening he would get a fever. Several *kabiraj* doctors had come and given him *Ayurvedic* medicine. Nothing worked. I felt even more worried and scared watching Gypsy, our german shepherd. She lay quietly all day long, keeping her face down with droopy ears, on her stretched out limbs next to Babu's bed. Gypsy refused to eat anything either. Dogs sometimes feel and understand better than we do, and that was what worried me more. Why was Gypsy acting like that?

Padma came one day and brought her father. As soon as Dr. Kader Choudhury entered, a wide smile shone on Babu's face. The salt and pepper bristles on Babu's unshaven face could not hide how thin he had become in a week.

"Look at you! What have you done to yourself?" the doctor picked up Babu's wrist while trying to cheer him up. The dog stood up and looked at the doctor wagging her tail.

"Yes, yes, I'll make him better, Gypsy. Don't you worry," he cuddled her throat.

Dr. Kader gave Babu a shot and some medicine. "Here is a prescription for some more. How come you did not call me before, my friend? Now, you rest. I'll check on you soon." He handed Babu the prescription.

Babu got better within a few days and Dr. Kader was invited for tea. While munching on the fresh homemade samosas he asked me,

"So, Srimati, how's your rehearsal going? Did you submit your parent's consent form?"

I am no Srimati. Did Padma tell him about dancing with my own shadow? Do they gossip and make fun about my make-believe world? My dream—my secret? I felt angry first, then shy and self-conscious.

"I don't think it will work for me. My parents will not like me dancing on the stage in public. So I did not try." I kept twirling my fingers gazing at the floor.

"What? What makes you think that? It is a rare once-in-a-lifetime opportunity. You'll remember about this precious experience forever. Why would your parents take that away? Silly girl!" He turned to Babu and my grandfather.

"What are you talking about, I have no clue?" Babu squinted at me.

Uncle Kader, Padma and I tried to explain the whole thing while Dr. Kader added that this year there had been a gathering of the Muslim League where a prominent political leader talked a lot about idol worshipping and that might have reflected in the school this year, otherwise every year in the past, students did participate in events on Saraswati Puja. Everyone joined them.

After that my grandfather drew me close and held my chin, "I thought you only dance in our courtyard, my precious child, in front of your own shadow. Now you'll be dancing on real stage? Hope you do not forget to invite me!"

At that moment I ran to get the paper and my father's signature shimmered on it.

*   *   *

While I was busy getting my form signed, Padma disappeared. *Where did my friend go?* I found her in the other room surrounded by my relatives, the five religious Hindu widows.

Auntie Asha was their captain. Her salt and pepper hair tied in a tiny bun at the top of her head, she carried a duster on her shoulder. She did not consider anything clean enough so she had this compulsion of dusting and wiping everything herself. She trusted her own duster only, the red and white checkered *gamcha*.

Auntie Asha showed her prized possession, a box. The box was full of tiny bottles that had water. She collected water from different parts of the holy Ganges River.

"Here, this is from *Gomukh*, where Ganga is just a baby, just born," she whispered. She handed another vial that read *Alakananda*.

"Ganga is here a little girl, hopping, skipping, playing hopscotch on the pebbles and stones to make her way. Here she is a teenager, her name is now *Mandakini*. Same Ganga, just various stages. See! Now here Ganga meets the Brahmaputra!" Her voice deepened.

A ray of sunlight shone on Padma's face. I could see that she was listening with wide eyes, fascinated by the holy Ganga stories.

Then, auntie Asha declared that where there is no Ganges River, like our region, you may get the same benefit taking a dip in the Brahmaputra River. But how would ladies from fine aristocratic, Hindu Brahmin families take a bath with everyone? In those cases, the solution was a *palki*, palanquin.

The ladies would sit in a covered palanquin which the bearers would take to the river and immerse in the water. That way you get a group bath with your fellow people without mixing with common folks. Padma was excited. "May I join too?" She exclaimed.

"Of course you may." Auntie Asha squeezed her cheeks. "What a sweet, religious girl!"

They decided next Sunday would be the best day for this outing. After Padma left, Auntie Asha asked,

"What is that girl's last name? Is she our caste? She'd be just perfect for my youngest son."

"Padma is Muslim, Auntie." I replied.

Auntie Asha jumped across the room. "What? And you let her sit beside me, touch all my holy waters?" She started dusting and scrubbing ferociously everything that touched my friend, with a little checkered cloth duster. She hurried to take a shower as if she was splashed with dirty sewer water.

She gathered all her belongings muttering that she would not spend a single day in this polluted environment.

"How could you let your child play with a Muslim girl like that?"

She barked at my mother.

"She is her best friend. And Padma's father is my husband's best friend too. He is the doctor who cured him, saved my husband's life. You saw that." Mother replied.

This is the first time I saw my mother standing up refusing to give in to their weird whims. I felt proud of her. Next day, Sunday, when the rickshaws came instead of the palanquins and our guests left with their bags and baggage, Ma was sorry. She started sniffling. She did not want it to end like that, after all that hard work of hospitality. She had tried so hard to make them feel welcome in our home. And it all failed at the end. She kept wiping her tears when my grandfather appeared. "Good riddance!" his deep voice bellowed and that made Ma burst into laughter.

*   *   *

Monday we found that some of the girls who had important roles in the dance drama did not have approvals from their guardians. Ashmani was one. Several girls who had permission took turns to dance for her to keep the continuity in the rehearsals. At one time it was my turn to fill in for Ashmani.

After school Bokuldi, our teacher called me aside. "Would you like to do Srimati's role? It is a lot of commitment but we felt that you may be able to make it if you try hard. What do you think?"

I could not believe my ears. Blood rushed on my cheeks, I could sense the heat. "I'll give all it takes, Bokuldi." I ran to Padma to give her the news.

Day and night I worked, for the next few days, every day. The dance teacher worked equally hard with me. She gave me all she could and I devoured it.

On the performance night, they dressed me up. A sheer gold

organza sari draped my body, decked with all kinds of unusual jewelry a court dancer would wear.

Long seven-strand necklaces of *navaratna*—nine precious stones, adorned me. Kundan chandeliers dangled from my ears. A long tikli with crystal beads dazzled the parting of my hair underneath the tiara. Silver snakes embellished my bare forearms. *Ratanchur* shone on my five fingers attached with delicate chains to hold my wrists and then there were *nupurs* tied on my ankles that jingled as I walked.

After the hairdo and the makeup they brought me in front of the large mirror. Who is this? Me? I could not believe it. It looked like the model girl on the calendar! I felt proud and shy at the same time.

On stage it was an enchanting experience, an evening full of magic and awe. I was transported to a different era, mesmerized to be transferred to a different persona. My make-believe world scintillated around me. The curtain dropped. Hundreds of voices exclaimed, encore! encore!. I was pushed to appear again and again in front of the curtain while people clapped with "Bravo Srimati, bravo! *kyabath! Kyabath!*" Bouquets of flowers showered on to me. I had never felt so high in my life.

In the green-room students and teachers came to congratulate. Padma was the first one. She hugged and kissed me and I could hear the same drumming in her heart. Bokul di came and grabbed my hand. "Quickly come out. There is a very special visitor, a very honored guest waiting to meet Srimati in person." She hissed.

It was the Assistant District Magistrate's wife. Madam held my hands. "Congratulations. I have seen this done by professionals, but you were no less than them tonight. You are very talented and beautiful. If you ever need anything do not hesitate to come to me." Then after a pause added, "Even if you need nothing, just come sometimes." She smiled at Bokuldi and me.

Uncle Kader was right. I'd never forget this night, ever in my life. Madam's words echoed over and over in my mind.

*   *   *

As I was getting ready to go home, I saw something. A person covered in a black cloak.

It was Ashmani. Her face covered in a black shawl, only the eyes twinkled. Her dark, big eyes filled with tears. *Did she come to say something? What is that?*

Our eyes were fixed on each other and I felt that mine were welling up too, everything getting blurry. My lips quivered. I wanted to tell her…

She fled. Ran away in the darkness somewhere. I realized she must have been forbidden to come here tonight, anyway.

Ashmani, you gave me this gift today. It was your passion that ignited the inspiration in me. I never knew what dancing was before I saw you. You taught me without knowing. This is all yours, all the attention and compliments I got tonight. You deserved it. Not me. You are the Pujarini.

But it was all unsaid.

The star-kissed night wore a veil of thick darkness now, chanting:

> *my heart trembles in pain*
> *ripples bob in the ocean of peace.*

10

GROWING PAIN

One Sunday morning when I was in the study doing my homework I was startled by the screech of tires. I opened the wooden shutters and saw a car was just parked near our portico. A dark navy blue car, square framed with silver accents, and a cream canvas on the top. The headlights resembled two eyes, wearing round spectacles and as if on its mouth it had a shy grin. It was beautiful, something I had never seen before.

A gentleman got out. He wore a long black coat even in that warm weather, a top hat, and had a cigar in his mouth. I watched as he banged the door shut and pranced up the stairs.

I could not see any more from my window but sensed by the excited chatter a commotion within the house. I could tell Ma and Babu were both thrilled to see him and I ran down to be introduced. He was my Sahib Kaku- a distant uncle who had just returned from England. Ma got busy in the kitchen, cooking, adding extra special impressive dishes to the lunch menu but Sahib Kaku only picked up a glass of coconut water and shoved away all the rest. Politely he admitted that he had dropped the native habit of eating big lunches and these days ate only fruits and nuts in the daytime, to stay fit.

I could see that my father felt a bit embarrassed being so full, rubbing his full belly, yawning and getting ready for an afternoon nap; a side pillow in his hand, while Sahib Kaku chuckled, "Come on, let's go check out the Bagan Bari (Garden House) estate." His eyes twinkled. "Ha'bout that ?" he added with British intonation. Then he swiftly turned to me "Young lady, h'bout you too?"

I was excited that he referred me as 'young lady' and ran to Ma to inform her about this invitation. She was hesitant. I started nagging, "Why can't I go? When will I ever have a chance to ride a car like that? I am sick of the boring *tongas* and phaetons with horses that smell. Why do you Ma always make everything forbidden to me?"

"What would you do there all alone? When I go you come with me too, okay?" she tried to convince. This was when Babu entered the room. "Well, I think it's not a bad idea. After all, it is polite for children to visit their relatives, especially the old ones. Did you hear that his mom is bedridden now? It will cheer her up."

I had never seen a car like that before, not to mention riding in it. Sahib Kaku showed us how the hood could be folded and that is why it is called a convertible. The name of the car was the Ford Coupe convertible and indeed it was a Deluxe model. I made a mental note of all this for I'd need that while bragging about it to Padma soon.

Sahib Kaku opened the door for me with a chic bow and offered me to sit first in the front. Then he went around to the driver's seat. No chauffeur! How thrilling. He was so modern. Everything about him had such a foreign, exotic flair. He smelled like a sweet expensive cigar, not the sweaty cigarette kind of cheap thing. His confident gait, the French cut beard, the way he held the cigar between two fingers and let it burn and waste, seemed so stylish. Especially I loved the way he addressed me, treating me as a young lady.

We soon came to learn that his passion was hunting. As we entered his mansion, a huge stuffed Royal Bengal Tiger greeted us at the corner of the porch. Another skinned one was lying on the floor as a rug. There were antlers on the doorways. Animals' heads decorated the walls. With an ornate baton, he pointed to one of those, "Have you any idea what kind of creature this is?"

We shook our heads though I thought it looked like a cow or a buffalo.

"It is a Nilgai—a wild animal of Tibet."

"Really!" We were astonished.

"Yes, it has a funny story. When I hunted it and brought it home, you know what the ladies said? They would not cook a cow. 'We are in a Hindu home, aren't we?' I had to convince them. *Arre baba*, it's more close to a deer family, nothing to do with a cow! Oh the ignorance of our women in this country! It's a shame, I tell you… and what can you expect from a nation where the leader is a naked fakir?"

I saw Babu's jaw drop. "Are you talking about Bapuji? Gandhi?"

Uncle was a bit taken aback looking at Babu's gaping, hurt face and quickly changed the subject. "And this fellow gave me trouble," he poked his baton at a gigantic, stuffed black bear that was standing in another corner. I turned to look again and couldn't help evading its eyes. I saw they were glaring with rage.

After passing down the long veranda we found ourselves in a room which was quite dark and filled with all kinds of dark mahogany wood furniture. A strange smell of medicine and Dettol (cleaning solution) overwhelmed the air. An old lady lay supine in an ornate large bed from which she could not get up, being totally paralyzed. I greeted her with *namaskar* and then heard Babu saying to me, "Khukumoni, you stay here with your Thama (grandma). Jump up on the bed here chat and have a good time. We'll be back soon." Everything was quiet for a long while then the lady spoke, "So, how are you?"

"Fine, thank you."

"What did you eat for lunch today?"

"Fish curry and rice."

"Hmm." Another long silence. I kept my hands folded on my lap trying to be polite but found that my legs started swinging impatiently from that high bed. Studying the designs on the wooden posts and running my fingers on the carved vines and roses I killed some time. Yet, I felt claustrophobic, stuffy and jittery.

"*O ma go*…, where are you!" she whined with deep sighs.

"Yes, m'am?" I responded.

"Oh, it's you. So how are you?"

"I am okay. Thank you." I tried to remember my manners.

"What did you eat for lunch today?"

I felt quite eerie now. *Who lives in this huge haunted house I thought. Is she all alone here?* I looked up. A lizard on the wall was staring at me with bulging eyes and then swiftly caught a moth. I shivered and turned away. But it had a hypnotic power. I had to look again, and this time saw how it was gulping the whole moth.

I climbed down from the high bed and to my surprise found some interesting objects inside a glass *almirah*. Walking closer I saw the most beautiful dolls and figurines inside. There was one porcelain doll with pale ivory skin and she was holding a golden flute close to her pink lips. Her fingers were thin and tiny; everything about her was delicate and dainty, even her eyes had long lashes.

Another statue caught my attention. I stepped out of the dark room to the adjoining veranda where an octagonal Burmese teak stool held a statuette. I had never seen such a thing in my life. Is this how memsahibs (western white women) look? Her skin was snow white, and she had golden hair that cascaded down her back. She was naked. Almost. Her right hand was on her bosom and her left holding a lock of her cascading hair covered her private parts. She was standing on a colossal shell, eyes looking far away. So beautiful. It mesmerized me until I sensed something uncanny.

As I turned, I saw a man at the end of the veranda staring at me. He was not far away. Muscles bulging from his sleeveless undershirt, this hairy, ebony man, wearing a dirty red and white checkered *lungi* was grinning and gesturing me to come close. Ugh! I turned away pretending not seeing him. But now I could sense that he was closer. Really close, maybe just behind. I dared not turn my face. I could feel his warm, moist, sultry breath falling on my nape, on my shoulder. His hands were on my waist, creeping up and down. I felt ticklish and numb at the same time.

He captured me from the back in a tight embrace like a sleazy python. Something hard was poking and pushing into me. His fingers were crawling under my skirt. He started kissing my nape moving my hair, murmuring "You are prettier now, ummm, Do you remember me? We met at that Mohim's shop?" I tried to scream, but found I had no voice. I felt dizzy. My mouth was dry and everything was spinning around me.

All of a sudden I lost balance and toppled. With the right heel of my shoe I stepped on his bare big toe and smashed it with all my weight. He lost his balance. As soon as I found he had fallen, I kicked him with all my strength and spat on his face. I ran inside and stood as close as I could to the body of this old lady who was totally paralyzed.

"Oh you! You are back? Did you see the animals?"

"Yes!" I sighed. "When is my father coming back?"

"Oh, he'll come. You are fine here, aren't you? So, what did you eat for lunch today?"

* * *

When Babu and Sahib Kaku came back he gave us a ride back home. That beast who had attacked me came to see us off. Sahib kaku introduced him to Babu, "This is Aziz, our caretaker." The man nodded with a salaam. When the car swerved out of the portico, my uncle added:

"Without him I would be lost. He takes care of everything, my mother, petty problems with the estate… I leave everything to him when I have to travel. When the river bends and land appear on one side or goes under the river's belly at another time, we zaminders face big confusion. You know how it goes, regarding the possession of the land, right? Once there was a big fight and my cousin, the other heir of the property, sent people to claim it. I said no. Now it is on my side. My area. Too bad the river moved away and ate up your part. This fertile land is mine… I am not giving it up. It did not work. He sent another agent. Then I sent Aziz. He took care of it. With one swing of his stick on the head that was all it took. Then he put the corpse in a sack with pebbles and stones and just dropped it in the river. It was all Aziz's idea. Clean job. The river gulped it. Since then, there is no problem. I told Aziz, you have my permission to take care of such things when I am not around.

SHADOW BIRDS

Now, you know that I have to travel out of the country quite a bit these days. I go to England frequently. He takes care of everything, my mother, petty problems with the estate. I leave everything to him. He is a great *lathial (stick player)*, so far undefeated. Can you believe that? So people fear him too, you know..." Shaheb Kaku burst out in a guffaw.

I shivered and stared out the window.

11

A LOVE STORY

A creek ran through our neighborhood. Right in front of our house it became a little lake, *Kachdighi*—the Glass Lake, we called it. I went there often through the back door of our garden and sat on the set of steps, dipping my ankles in its cool water. Women from the neighborhood came to fill up their brass vessels and I would listen to the gossips of the town through their chattering.

One day two little boys had a fight over a kite and their mothers during their quarrel, disclosed a juicy scandal that ran through generations. In time the argument stopped, the jabbering faded. Doves cooed *uhuhuhu… doob-doob-doob*. A white egret stood on one foot while three *pankauri* and a whole group of little coots dipped their heads to catch water-snails. A thin stream of water purled through the cracks of stones. Bubbles bobbed. By and by the afternoon grew quieter until it was absolutely still.

Ripples and rings around my ankles stretched away until there was nothing but thick mossy green pebbles, tiny and smooth, under my toes. The water was crystal clear. I nodded down and looked at my reflection. I gazed at it. *Will I ever find love? Someone, who will hold this face in his palms and…*

"*A*yee little sister!" It startled me. A *rickshaw wallah was* talking to me. "Do you know Bhabani babu's house?"

"He is my dad." I showed him how to go around to the front of the house and I ran through the garden to greet them at the portico.

Two women in the rickshaw, descended carefully. One grandmotherly lady with silver-white hair tied in a little bun and the other one was much younger, even younger than Ma.

My parents were overjoyed to see them. They introduced the older lady to me as grandma Dhuli (Dhuli didimoni, I should call her). I came to know that she had helped my mom to be born, and not only that, I was also born into her hands. She was the one who cut the cord for me. Dhuli didimoni was a midwife I understood, and the other lady, Buri didi (sister Buri) was her assistant. They traveled together and helped out pregnant mothers in our extended family. On their way to a neighboring village, they stopped to visit us for a few days.

Buri didi made me curious. Though she called Dhuli didimoni, Mamoni (mother dear), she was not her real mother. Then who was she? How come they lived together, traveled together? Was Buri didi married?

One day I asked Ma to get the answer. "You are very nosy and precocious. You are a little girl. Why don't you be like that?" she answered.

"Didn't you just mention the other day that you were married at my age, at thirteen, and I am way too childish?" I answered back.

She did not like that "Khuku, I told you many times not to talk back like that with grownups. It's not polite. You must learn these things." That was the end of that from Ma.

So Padma and I tried to keep our antennas open to find out the answer.

"Is she married? Does not look so. She does not wear the

auspicious *sindoor* (vermillion powder) dot on her forehead or at the parting of her hair, like all Hindu wives. Nor does she wear any iron wedding bracelet on her left wrist. If she is not married she could be a widow who lost her husband in childhood. But that does not seem plausible either. She does not live the life of a typical widow maintaining a vegetarian diet and wearing white clothes. Buri didi relishes fish and loves to wear colorfully printed saris. Society would not have tolerated that," I told Padma.

"Then, she could be a spinster. Maybe she had some kind of women health problems that prevented her from getting married," commented Padma.

"I would not believe that. A woman of that age does not have that choice. She would have fallen into the married category, in that case, either returned by her husband or kept as a servant for manual labor," I argued back.

So what was her story?

*　　　*　　　*

It was a quiet afternoon of the monsoon month of *Shaban*. We were up on the rooftop terrace garden, Buri didi, Padma and I, while the rest of the family were downstairs taking a nap after lunch.

Freshly laundered saris swayed in the air, drying at one corner. Several jars of *aachar* (pickles and chutneys) were basking in the sun, soaked in mustard oil. We stretched ourselves out on a wide straw mat, cozy with cushions and pillows. Padma and I were working on a complex beading project, stringing tiny glass beads and cowries to make a necklace, while Buri didi was busy sorting tiny stones from the lentils.

Dark, water-filled clouds hung on one side, but the sun shone too. It's rays played peek-a-boo with the leaves of the trees casting polka dot designs of light and shade. Far away the washermen were beating clothes on the stone in rhythmic thuds. The air smelled of fresh *kadom* blossoms.

Buri didi fixed her gaze far away, flung a piece of stone from the lentil mixture, and said;

"It was a day just like this, filled with the smell of *kadom* flowers... '*Badal diner prothom kodom phool*' the first *kadom* flower of the monsoon day." She hummed a tune, then paused taking off her glasses, and wiping her eyes with the corner of her sari.

"How old was I then? Maybe a few years older than you, just sixteen. What did I know of life?

"We went to visit Kolkata, to see my uncle's family. Kolkata, for the first time. Full of alleyways, narrow streets, cobblestone paths, tall houses. Houses, two and three stories tall. It was not open and wide like we have it here, dear.

Bottle-green colored iron railings surrounded the verandas. Dark green windows with wooden shutters and stained glass arched over, filtering yellow and orange lights. The floors were of black-and-white marble with diamond-shaped tiles. I had never seen such fancy, such extravagance in my life. We went to attend a wedding. This was my first experience of observing a whole wedding." Buri didi plucked a flower and pulled its petals.

"My cousin, Taru da was getting married. Early in the morning the women of the family blew conches and made a big fuss waking Taru da up. The *dadhimongol* ceremony had to be performed. 'Get up mister groom. It is your only chance to eat today before the sun rises until you take the wedding vows in front of the fire. Mind you!' They brought a big pot of dessert, a concoction of yogurt, *khoi*, (rice crispy) and sandesh (a dish made of sweet cream cheese). The ladies hollered, 'Who wants to taste it?' They found me in the front and gave me a handful. Oh, was it yummy!" Buri didi licked her lips in remembrance.

"Suddenly everyone cheered 'It's Mrinalini, it is Mrinalini, she will be the next one to be wed.' I came to learn that it is believed that the first person who tastes this concoction after the bride or groom, is the next one to be married."

"Mrinalini, is that your name, Buri Didi? So beautiful," I interrupted.

"Yes, my real name is Mrinalini. When I was a little girl I happened to be a precocious little one. At least my grandma thought so. She used to call me *paka buri,* meaning ripe old woman. From then on my nickname became Buri—the old woman. Now no one knows my other beautiful name. Everyone calls me Buri—the old woman." She sighed and went back to her story.

"They all warned Taru da he'd have to fast until the wedding vows are taken."

I interrupted again. "Come on, men never fast before taking wedding vows. They cheat somehow. It is the women, the foolish girls who stay hungry all day long and pray." I let my opinion out.

"Khukumoni, you are right. Men don't. It is only us." Buri didi grinned.

"Tell us what happened after they proclaimed that it was you, to be the next bride," Padma reminded her.

"Who'd ever marry me? I was a poor girl raised by a single, widow mom, who had no income. I was not pretty either, just a plain, simple village girl. We did not dream of my wedding. It embarrassed me to be the center of attention." She sighed and we sighed with her.

"Then we got busy for the next festivity of the wedding, the *Gaye holud*. Again the women hurried, warning that time was running out. Taru da would be smeared with turmeric paste mixed with mustard oil before his bath. Four tiny banana trees were brought. *Alpana*, designs of vines were drawn on the ground. A *piri,* rectangular wooden slab was brought with pretty designs drawn on it, of something like two fish swirling, in an abstract art form. Taru da had to step on it. The women had fun smearing the paste on his face and bare body. They made ululu sounds with their tongue and they poured sacred water on him which had the blessings of the forefathers.

This paste had to go to the bride's house, with lots of gifts. A new sari, jewelry, baskets and trays filled with sweetmeats and nuts and a pair of fresh fish, dressed artistically. The women of the groom's house would put vermillion *sindur* and yellow turmeric to design the two fish, one as a man and the other as a woman. This is the time to flaunt your artistic flair, showing off what a talented family the bride is getting married into.

They would smear this auspicious paste onto the bride, in her home. This would be the first indirect touch of her would-be-husband. The bride would be coy, but thrilled inside and shiver when they would pour cold water onto her. She had not seen her husband yet. It would happen tonight." Padma and I shivered in anticipation. "Continue." We pleaded

"After an elaborate lunch, the time came when the groom had to go to the bride's place. Taru da wore a silk kurta with a gold border with pearl buttons and a dhoti. A *topor*, the typical wedding hat was put on him. The *topor*, made of *shola*, a simple water plant, snow white with delicate designs carved on it was very beautiful. But that white conical hat on every groom looks comical. So it did on Taru da too, and we laughed, but he had to wear it, anyway. Then he boarded a car decorated with flower garlands.

We dressed up in our best clothes. When we reached the bride's house they greeted us with blowing conches. The mother of the bride greeted the groom first. Then came the time for the bride to be brought out and her veil was hoisted. They dressed her in a red silk sari with gorgeous gold border and jewelry. The bride and groom exchanged their first glances and put garlands on each other, garlands made of tuberoses and petals of rose.

Everyone cheered, and blew conches. Then suddenly I noticed..." Buri didi stopped.

"What? What happened then?" We cried out.

Buri didi took a deep breath, "Someone was looking at me; a pair of eyes fixed on mine. I looked away. But not for long. Next time as I checked out of the corner of my eyes I found he was still staring, this time with a smile, a handsome young fellow with dark features. Blood swarmed on my cheeks. It felt hot. I glanced around to make sure if anyone else were noticing." Buri didi blushed. I touched her hand, "And then?"

"Later, I came to know that he was my aunt's youngest brother, a final year medical student, who attended the wedding like me. He was living in the same house.

I stayed on to help my aunt with household work. She suffered from acute arthritis, so going up and down the stairs to fetch this and that, tidying up the house was my job. Especially bringing the dried laundry from the roof terrace in the late afternoons, sorting it and taking things to different rooms was a big chore. This is where I met him, and we both started looking forward to these evening roof terrace meetings.

One day he presented me with something special. It was round like a marble, dark brown in color, and when I put it in my mouth it was bittersweet, gradually melting with a heavenly taste. 'What is it?' I asked. 'Never had a chocolate before?' he laughed. 'I am a village girl. Where would I find such a modern, western delicacy?'

'Silly girl, you have a lot to learn,' he giggled and then he held my face and brought his down, touching his lips to mine. I flushed. My whole body trembled. I rushed downstairs.

The next few days I picked up the dry clothes much earlier, or later, at different times, making sure he was not there, to avoid him. Another part of me pined, dying to meet him, ravenous, begging to have that bittersweet experience again. At quiet times the experience of the first kiss played over and over in my mind. His first admiring glance was the gift for my sweet sixteenth year of life. It gave new meaning to my life. I felt so thankful to him. He had given me so much, but what did I have to give to him? I did not even dare to tell him all that I felt."

Buri didi paused a moment gazing into the distance. Her voice was soft.

"One day I found myself sewing the first letter of his name on an old handkerchief of his. I did not have much chance to go to school but I was good at embroidery. People said so.

The next day no one was at home. Uncle and Aunty went to visit a temple. Taru da and his new bride went out to a party. I had a feeling he had joined them too.

It was hot and muggy. I went up to the roof terrace to get some fresh air. It was a monsoon day of *Sraban*. The sun had gone down a little while before and in the twilight the *Saptarshi Mandal,* the seven-star constellation hung like a big question on the celestial sky. The air was filled with *Kadom phool* fragrance. I felt a touch on my back. It was him. He said nothing. Just kissed me. 'I'll leave tomorrow in the early morning first train, back to my college.' His salty tears mixed with love embraced my whole self. I couldn't breathe. I held my breath.

We lost ourselves in each other. We did not talk about our future, if we would ever be together, how we could keep in touch, none of these. All we knew was that those moments existed, and we wanted to hold on to them as tight as we could. They were quicksilver, magical moments. We gave everything we had to each other as a man and a woman. The sky filled up with millions of stars and they witnessed our union.

After he left I felt miserable, not just mentally, but physically too. A few weeks passed. I still didn't feel like eating and threw up each morning. Felt exhausted and tired all the time. All I wanted was to be left alone and sleep. And before I understood anything Aunty figured it out.

'You spoiled witch!' she screamed at me. 'You came to ruin my brother's life. You seduced him. You whore, is this how your mother trains you?' Aunty took me to *Kashi*. (Benaras), where it is believed that all destitute souls find a place in the temple, under *Baba Biswanath's* feet." Padma gripped my hand.

"The last months of my pregnancy Aunty ordered me to be dressed like a Hindu married girl with *sindoor* and all, so that it would be easy to find a rented home. Who'd rent a house to a person with an unwed pregnant woman?

There I gave birth to a beautiful little girl. Aunty took me to the temple. As ordered, I offered the baby on the feet of Baba Biswanath. She'd be taken to an orphanage, they told.

I cried and cried and prayed. *Keep an eye on her, Baba. Give her a good, loving home and Baba, one more wish; may I be able to see her father just one more time in my life?*

I handed the baby over to a woman of the ashram. She was wearing a white sari with a thin blue border. Her face looked kind.

After we returned Aunty threw a package onto my lap. Inside there was a similar white sari with thin blue border and some money. 'Take off your sindoor, you are no one's wife. Get lost, go to your village to your mother if you have the guts, or whatever.' She left leaving me there, all alone." I felt a tear run down my cheek.

Buri di started, "My mother came to see me. 'Fate of being a poor woman' she cried, but could not bear this pain for too long and she died. After I cremated her. I sat on the bank of River Ganga, sobbing, *Father show me some signs, give me some direction. What should I do? Where shall I go?* Then I fell asleep exhausted until a lady shook me awake.

'Come with me, my child, there is always room for one more in my home. Stay with me until you are healed, until you are ready, stay as long as you wish.' It was Mamoni."

Buri didi took off her glasses to wipe away her tears.

Drops of water fell from the celestial sky too. Dark clouds gathered, and the wind picked up. We hurried to collect the dry clothes and the jars of pickles.

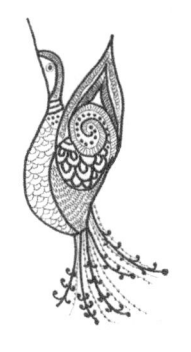

12

MIGHTIER THAN A SWORD

"You don't know how privileged, how lucky you are that today you can go to school. We did not have that privilege. Never neglect your studies." Dhuli didimoni summoned.

Which thirteen-year old child likes to hear such lectures? We didn't either.

But when we heard, "Just a stroke a of pen, and that saved my life," we sat up straight.

"How? How was your life saved? Tell us, tell us." Padma's doe-eyes twinkled. Dhuli didimoni cackled, "Oh that's a long story. You must go back to your studies now. Prepare for your exams."

"Please, please Didimoni, we'll stay up late tonight and catch up for our tests, now tell us that story, please," we cuddled beside her.

"Well, then listen." She opened the lid of a brass box. The rectangular ornate box had several chambers inside. Dismantling, we found that the very first one was a shallow tray that held a moistened cloth. Dhuli didimoni gently took out the tray and put it aside. Unfolding the moist cotton cloth she took out a betel leaf, *paan*. Several tiny cylindrical brass pots came out after that. From the very first one, she scooped out a little white paste, slaked lime, and smeared it onto the *paan* with the tip of her forefinger. She added areca nut pieces, *supari*, from the second one and then from the very last one she drew out a pinch of silvery something and added on her *paan*. "This is *zarda*, a kind of sweet tobacco, absolutely not okay for kids. It will make your head spin like crazy and make you throw up and that'd be the proof that you stole *zarda* and ate it." She warned with wide eyes. Didimoni then folded the *paan* into a neat triangle and shoved it in her mouth. One side of her cheek flared up as she kept on chewing.

We knew it would be a long wait now until that puffed cheek normalizes. The little pots and pans went back to the brass box to their respective designed space. She shut the lid with a swift click. Didimoni swallowed the juice of her *paan* with great relish and started:

"I was the fifth child of the ten children my parents had. But the very first daughter. I had three younger sisters. When I was nine years old, I was married. Remember little of that, only, that I was bundled in a heavy red sari with a thick gold border. Real gold thread. They hung gold jewelry on me that were too heavy and bulky for my size. I felt like a sack, but fell asleep anyway. Late at night, they woke me up, carried, and took me to the groom. I had no idea how the man looked, or what this fuss was all about. All I remembered was, I had overheard a whispering murmur, 'Oh, what a match, such a beautiful girl for that old coffin-dodger? How long is he going to last?'

'Hush, hush, think, what a family she is going to be married to, the highest of the Brahmin caste, a *Kulin Brahmin*. They have three more daughters to be married and this will pave their paths.'

'Doesn't the groom have fourteen other wives?' someone remarked. 'Of course he does. Which *Kulin Brahmin* groom would you find that doesn't?' another answered.

'Why you frown, dear child. Smile. It's your wedding today,' an old lady held up my chin with a toothless grin. I must have scowled and turned away, I don't remember.

I lived with my parents for four more years. But then came a day when I became a woman, and it was time to go to my husband's house.

I vividly remember that day. I had heard that my husband was almost my father's age. To me he looked like my grandfather and indeed he had fourteen wives.

All my family came to see me off at the river bank. While they were busy with the farewell rituals, I looked around. The sky was crisp cerulean, not a single speck of cloud. A blue *machranga,* kingfisher bird, with its long scarlet beak gazed faraway. An egret stood on one leg, forever. The *swarna champa* tree was full of blossoms. Tiny bell-shaped, golden flowers made an amber circle around the tree. People walked on them, trampled, unaware. Unaware of that heavenly smell.

That smell defined home to me. My childhood, my familiar life, all that I was leaving here.

Ulululu. I startled at that shrill. They were now inaugurating me, ceremoniously saying goodbye, wishing me a safe journey to my new life. Clay lamps were lit, they smeared sandalwood paste on my forehead. A man from the groom's team announced that we must hurry, speed things up. My younger sister, Bonu, scurried. Streaks of tears running down her cheek, she embraced me in a tight hug and emptied something from the corner of her sari to mine. And then tied a tight knot to keep the contents safe. The *swarna champa* flowers. Some spilled on my feet. *How could she know?*

They pushed me to board the boat. The rope unfurled. The vessel shook. I felt dizzy as if there was no ground under my feet. Indeed, there was none. I held on to those flowers as tight as I could to my bosom. They were the only tie with my known world.

*   *   *

The following winter my husband died. My life started a new chapter. Widowhood. All the rituals of a pure Hindu widow. No colors to wear, nothing other than a vegetarian diet to eat, no happy functions to take part in.

My job was to take care of the children. We had a big family with many kids. Children of all sizes and shapes. Babies of the fourteen wives my husband had left. Preparing food for them, keeping that kitchen in order, was my job. And yes, there was another thing I learned, the job of a midwife. Though I did not have any child of my own, I came to know all about it very well.

In those days women were not allowed to touch books. It was believed that touching printed words, even seeing them would bring bad luck. It will shorten the husband's life. In my case, this superstition made little sense. My husband was already dead. What could I risk losing?

When the boys did their homework; studied, and practiced their letters and numbers on their chalkboards, I carefully watched them. When they forgot and left their books in the kitchen, I studied them and practiced those letters. With black coal from the stove, I practiced the letters and the numbers over and over on the kitchen floor and then gushed it out with water, with vigorous scrubs. Nobody knew because there was no trace, no proof of anything.

One day I got caught. Little Nitai, just ten years old, glimpsed that I was reading. He was amused that I tried to read and I, an old adult woman is interested in his books. He cuddled close to me and corrected me when needed.

Nitai and I made a secret deal that afternoon that I'd give him extra help for making his kites and he'd give me lessons. He was interested to be my tutor and promised that we'd both keep it private. Within a short time, I caught up to his level. I learned how to write my name. I could do simple math and understand the printed messages.

After the month of *Sraban* that year, monsoon started, and it rained. It drizzled, and showered and poured for fourteen days. Thunder bolted. Clouds burst and the torrential rain drained us. For fourteen days it rained and rained. The village flooded. Ripened harvest bowed down. The granary sunk. Water bobbed up from the ground drowning the cowshed. Cattle swam, floated and eventually sank, dead. Animals and pets died.

People erected poles and logs to scaffold and save human lives. My precious possessions, whatever little I had, a bit of gold, some money, clothes in the trunk floated away. The rest sank somewhere. We just held our children and dear ones and prayed for the rain to stop.

One day it did. The sun shone in the clearest blue sky, shameless and happy as if nothing had happened. Heaps of dead, decayed animals and debris were all that was left.

Then came cholera. There was so much water the other day, and now not a drop to drink. People died left and right. There were not enough people or energy to cremate or bury the dead. Young people started fleeing. Everyone wanted to leave this dreadful place. We women, had no choice, our hands were tied to destiny.

Even Nitai was leaving in search of fortune in the towns, in the cities. I wiped off my tears and cleaned whatever was left. And to my surprise, I found his first book, a pen, some paper, soaked, dried, wrinkled and an ink-pot with the lid tightly shut.

A strange feeling engulfed me. I picked up one of those papers, and the pen and held them to my bosom. I prayed to the Goddess Saraswati, the goddess of learning. *Please, Mother, help me. Come to the tip of my pen and bless me, Ma.*

I felt tears rolling down my face. I took a deep breath, opened the ink-pot and dipped the quill. I saw that I have written: *Dear Father, Wherever you are please rescue me. I am still alive.* Then I signed my name. That was my first experience in writing.

I gave the piece of paper to Nitai and asked him to please visit my village and give it to my father.

Several months passed. Then one day a young man of Nitai's age came and knocked at our door. He asked for me. The man explained that he was coming from my childhood village, from the zaminder. My father had died in the meantime, and the family was scattered, my parent's village was also hit hard with the epidemic cholera and famine. But my letter reached the zaminder's hand somehow. This zaminder was your grandfather. He arranged to fetch me.

This was when your mom was about to be born. The baby

survived but shortly after that your grandmother passed away leaving the newborn infant. I took care of your mom until she was five years old. In the meantime, my name as a midwife spread all over. Whenever a baby was to be born, they called me.

Life takes strange bends, like a river. That one-line-letter made all the difference in my life."

13

FORBIDDEN

When I was in Babu's library, late at night, buried under thick Trigonometry books and papers, everybody thought I was preparing for my upcoming tests. I was reading a novel, a forbidden book, *Bishabriksha* (The Poisoned Tree).

I had heard about this book from older girls while riding the school bus, eavesdropping in their conversation that this was hot stuff. When I discovered it in my own house, in Babu's bookshelf, I could not resist myself. But I knew that it was not for me. It was kept high up, on the highest shelf, locked with Babu's other important stuff. I was forbidden to open that shelf.

But I did. And I was thoroughly immersed in the life of Kunda, the thirteen-year-old orphan who comes into the lives of a happily married couple Nagendra and Suryamukhi. When the orphan adolescent, Kunda, becomes a widow, Surya (Nagendra's wife), out of the goodness of her heart opens their home to her. Surya and Kunda grow a bond of friendship. Tension arises when Surya's husband gets attracted to Kunda and can not hide it.

Now and then my thoughts for these imaginary characters meandered into my daily life. I wondered, was it right that Kunda should never accept any one's admiration, attention or love for the rest of her life? What was it that was left for her in life? Was society not responsible for her situation? Was it she to blame because she was beautiful and had bad luck?

Kunda and Buri didi kept merging in my unconscious mind. But no one knew about it. All that was going on in my head remained hidden behind that desk, cluttered with the protractor and divider and thick geometry books.

I could not keep it all to myself and took it to my dear friend Padma. Padma's dark eyes grew wider. She showed interest in reading the forbidden book too. We agreed that we should take turns. One night she could keep the book and catch up, the next day we'd meet at the lakefront to exchange thoughts and the book too. The following day it'd be my turn to keep the book; in one condition, it had to be highly confidential and must be done with great secrecy. She understood that we'd both be in big trouble if they found us reading a forbidden book.

Padma came with tears streaking down her face when Nagendra failed to hide his attraction for Kunda, and Surya had to deal with their affair. Padma felt more for Surya than she did for Kunda, "Is this how you treat your wife's trust, her goodness?" she baffled.

I argued, "What could one do under such circumstance? Would Surya ever feel the same for her husband even if Kunda was removed from their lives. Yes, they may patch up as husband and wife but wouldn't their relationship be broken as lovers? Love is a mirror where you see your reflection; once broken, it is broken. Marriage is like an earthen pot. It holds you both. Once broken, you can fix it and it will hold, maybe." I giggled. We both stayed quiet, gazing at the water of the Glass Lake.

"Well said, my friend, did you read it somewhere?" Padma asked.

"No, just made it up, this very minute."

Then we took the book, and under the *shiuli* tree, stretched out upon the dropped blossoms and read together until the very last line.

Surya understands her husband's condition. She gives him the consent to marry Kunda. Nagendra suffers. He feels like a traitor, disloyal to his magnanimous wife's love, yet can not deny Kunda either. At the end, Kunda takes poison and kills herself.

"Phew! Coward writer and hopeless Nagendra!" I stood up.

"What else could the writer do with Kunda?" Padma defended. "Just imagine he had written this book sixty to seventy years from today, in eighteen something. How far have we come regarding the marriage of widows? The author, Bankim Chandra, was way ahead of his time. He acknowledged the feelings of Kunda, the helplessness of the girl; that is good enough for me.

"I loved the way he gave more prominence to this thirteen-year-old Kunda's beauty. Don't you feel so?" I looked into Padma's eyes..

"Weren't you checking the mirrors more than usual, I bet you did?" Padma beamed. But I need to check out a few things one more time, can I keep it tonight?" she pleaded.

"Just be careful." I agreed.

* * *

In a blink of eye the quaint, quiet corner of our lakefront changed into a raucous scene. Streets filled with people screaming, running, swearing. Some had sticks in their hands, some fire. "Inquilab Zindabad!" (long live the revolution) slogan hollered. The rickshaw pullers, their heads hanging on one side, woke up startled, from their lazy afternoon slumber. They gaped bewildered. The mob yelled, "Run. Escape. Riot!"

Doors of the shops banged shut. The giant *Ma Tara* grocery store slammed down its iron shutter with a loud thud.

A young boy whacked, beaten up, rolled on the ground in a bloody pool. A crowd swarmed, rushed to check him out. *I know that boy. Isn't that Abdul?*

We knew them all. Raja, Rahim, Abdul. They were friends playing marbles just the other day! The famous three musketeers we called them. They hung around in front of the grocery store when the soldiers came and tipped them chocolates. American and British soldiers often showed up to fill up their trucks with supplies and groceries from here and those street boys, regardless of their religion, Hindu or Muslim, took part in loading the trucks. They came looking forward to the tips from the soldiers. Then they shared the tips, chocolates, and candies. I had seen it. And today they were turned against each other, killing each other. *Why?*

Padma and I confused, stared at each other and gazed at the scenario. *Could friendship be this fragile?*

"What are you two doing here?" a voice bellowed. The car screeched in front of us and we were shoved in. It was Uncle Kader. There was a curfew that night, and we were prohibited to go anywhere. I was picked up with Padma and stayed in their house until things quieted down.

*   *   *

Where did the forbidden book go? I tried to find it wandering in our garden the next day. I could not find it anywhere. Then I remembered when I had seen it last. Did we leave it under the tree that day? Did Padma take it? I looked under the tree. No, it was not there. I looked for it behind all the bushes in our garden and then I met two shadows approaching. Dr. Kader and my friend, Padma, behind him. The book was tucked under Dr. Kader's arm.

"Where is your father? I thought I'd see him in his garden." Dr. Kader said.

"P... please may I have the book? I'll put it back in his library." I quailed.

"No, no, I can do that myself. Is he in his library?" He started walking towards the library. As we followed him, he turned to me, "Did you have time to finish the book? Did you like it?" I gave Padma a side glance. "We b... b... both read it" I answered with a downcast glance.

"I know. She was reading hiding it under her Geometry book. My point is what did you get out of it?" he looked at us.

After a while, Padma gushed it in one breath, "I kind of liked it. His language is rich, I think. It is beautiful though not easy. I had to check the dictionary a lot." Her response gave me courage.

"I think he was a good writer in bringing up Kunda's feelings, which our society would not accept." I added.

"Good. Good critical thinking. This means you both were ready for this book. Sometimes we don't know until we try."

We saw Babu entering the garden. Uncle Kader raised the book up and said, "These ladies managed to finish this book and I was telling them you never know if a book is good or bad unless you give it a try. Also, no books should be forbidden in my opinion. What do you think?" Babu was a bit perplexed to answer.

Dr. Kader started, "If you cannot understand or digest a book, it is not for you; rather, you are not ready for it. Anyway, I was thinking of taking them to the public library today and issue their library cards." Babu said, "I'm all for that. You have my permission to take my daughter to this sacred journey. Bon voyage."

*   *   *

Books, books, books. So many books, I was awestruck. From the ground up, the walls, there were shelves full of books. Narrow hallways filled with shelves, full of books, and a tall slim ladder to reach the very top ones. A cherry wood cabinet with narrow drawers and tiny shell buttons held the references. The librarian lady showed us how to find a book by title, subject or author's name, opening the slim drawers of the cabinet.

There were pictures and portraits of celebrated personalities on the wall. Like Queen Victoria, a western sahib with long hair and a high forehead wearing a lacy, frilly collar. I went closer and read William Shakespeare. *Oh! he is the writer who wrote Hamlet and Othello and The Merchant of Venice that we performed last year in school.* I was amused. Then I saw a picture of Bankim Chandra too, with his rolled hair dress resembling a candy cane with stripes. Sometimes while I read a book I wondered—how did the author look?

The best I liked was a large picture of two girls, teenagers, just like

Padma and me. One had long hair like Padma, part of it tied in a ribbon, like she did, and the other girl in red, with dark hair and a bit roundish face. She kind of resembled me, I thought. They were reading a book. They were really into it. *A forbidden one?* I went close to read the artist's name. Auguste Pierre Renoir. I did not know his name. But he touched me. Those girls were just like us, except they had white skin, and golden hair.

"I'll be in the other room. You have one whole hour to read anything you like." Uncle Kader whispered. I noticed that even though there were many people in this room, it is very quiet. The place had a tranquil, cool ambiance, comforting, like the touch of a clay pot that held cool water for hot days.

Smell of books was in the air. I pulled one from a low shelf. 'Little Women.' I got immersed in the lives of Jo and Meg; Beth and Amy. I felt I was more like Jo, though I wished I were like Beth, as generous as Beth.

Saturdays were library days, and I fondly looked forward to it. Here, I got introduced to Apu, the character of the young boy in *Pather Panchali. Apu was a boy and I, a girl, but how come we had so much in common?* I cried at his sorrows and laughed at his silliness; walked hand in hand with him, in his journey. I loved the part where the author described Apu's adolescent years.

One day as I was waiting for my requested book to come, I caught a glimpse of a bunch of yellow pencils in a cup, neatly sharpened, arrows pointing up. Inviting. Inviting me to write.

Write, write! chirped a yellow warbler hopping on the windowsill.

Oh, how I wish to be a writer, write like Louisa Alcott or Bibhutibhushan, I sighed.

The lady came back with my book. I felt embarrassed as if she could see my secret flash dream. I blushed and grabbed my book to leave.

*   *   *

When we reached Dr. Kader's residence that day, we met a gang of people. Some of the faces looked familiar. Mahim, the sweet maker, Rahmat Ali and that *lathial* Aziz.

"*Selam aleikum!*" they greeted the doctor.

"*Aleikum selam!*" he greeted back. "How are you all? What's up!"

"That's what we have come to discuss with you, doctor sahib. Are you aware of what happened yesterday?" Aziz stepped forward. "It was Friday. *Namaz* time. The sound of *azan* in the air. We were all down on our prayer mats. Then we heard a bunch of Hindus playing obscene *filmy gana (film songs)* in loudspeaker in a rickshaw, circling the mosque. The voice of *azan* faded in that obnoxious, loud noise. What is this? Is this country only for them? Do they have no respect for us, our religion?" Aziz demanded.

A smirk passed through Dr. Kader's face. "Didn't you guys slaughter their holy cows in front of the temple, just a week before? On *Shiva Ratri*? All those people, who fasted day and night came to pray and worship in the morning and found slaughtered cows swimming in a pool of blood at their temple courtyard, how do you think they felt? Was it showing respect for their religion?" Dr. Kader smacked back.

"Rahim-sahib, our great teacher, was giving lessons to your kids and you told him to get out of your house. Is it true?" Aziz charged back.

"It is true. I heard Rahim-sahib saying, those who do not eat cows, instead, worship them, they are nothing but stupid fools. Those who worship dolls and images they are *kafir*, not our kin, not our friends." Dr. Kader replied.

"Do you disagree, doctor sahib? Beef is food. What's wrong saying that? Do you know how insulted our respected Rahim sahib felt in front of those children?"

"I disagree with the fact that those who refuse to eat beef or worship idols are stupids or fools. I have many Hindu and Buddhist friends whose religious practices are different from ours. I don't want my children to feel that they are not our well-wishers, or not our friends. It is wrong to plant seeds of hatred and racism in children's mind. That is exactly what he was doing. And as a father, I have a responsibility to protect my children. That is why I reacted like that." Dr. Kader explained.

"It is in our scripture that there is only one Allah. Idol worshipping is wrong. Do you not follow your religion?" Aziz snapped back.

"Look, I am a doctor, a scientist. My religion is to heal people, to serve. There are messages of peace in every religion, including mine. But I have patients both Hindu and Muslim. I see the same color in their blood. No difference." Dr. Kader shook his head. "We are against each other in this religious business. I don't agree everything that the Hindus are doing, nor what we are doing to them. I focus on my duty as a doctor, curing people's diseases, that's all." Dr. Kader blew an exhausted sigh.

"You are a *mehman admi, a sheriff admi*, doctor sahib. You are our pride, a respected person in the society. We need your help, your support." Rahamat tried to ease things up. "We have a meeting tonight and we are inviting you to come."

"Sorry, I can't." The doctor shook his head, but dug into his pocket and scooped out some money.

Aziz stepped forward and grabbed his hand. "We don't want your money if you are not with us." He looked at him with knitted brows.

"Khun ka baat karte ho doctorsaab! Who khun maine bhi dekha. Awr phir dekhenge. Adaab doctor sahib fir milenge."

Then he turned to me- a slow but sharp glance from my head to toe and toe to my eyes. It froze me. As if that sleazy, slimy snake was licking again, and he was stripping me in front of all.

"Let's go." He turned and the gang followed him out.

14

GRAMOPHONE

One day uncle Kader and Babu brought a big box with a huge brass cone. Padma and I huddled to see what was it all about. There was a picture of a dog with black spots on its ears sitting straight in front of that ornate brass cone.

Music came out of it. Padma looked at me and grinned, it thrilled us to see what this thing could do. In the beginning, it was only a possession of Dr. Kader then later Babu bought one for our home too. In the meantime, Babu started a collection of records that he shared with the doctor.

There was Western music and Hindustani classical, Tagore's songs and Nazrul's, in that collection, but what caught me and my friend most was a folk song—*Hei samalo hei samalo*—an upbeat one, perfect for dancing.

Padma and I started humming, then sang in duet, harmonizing and making all kinds of improvisations. We found ourselves dancing to it. It had such a dynamic rhythm that we decided that we would choreograph it and put on a show, not caring who our audience would be.

"It must have jumps and skips like this." Padma leaped and pranced, flounced and bobbed clapping her hands with the beats.

"Yes, and the swings will be swift, quick and abrupt," I added, twirling my body, catching her hand and lifting it up in the air. We held each other's waists and kicked our legs with gusto.

"Remember, no dull, dopey, slow feet moves allowed, none of your dreamy poses, okay?" warned Padma. "Of course not." I assured her, hopping and skipping from one end of the courtyard to the other.

Now the dress. We decided to wear saris as the *Santal* (native folks, aboriginals) women would. Just plain cotton ones with bold primary color borders. We would put them high up showing off our calves, not modestly letting it hang down to our ankles, tightly wrapping it to our waist. No glittery gold jewelry. We chose simple chunky wooden beads made out of betel nuts (the fruit of the *supari* trees that we see around), coiled our hair to side-buns and tucked a vermillion hibiscus like the *Santal* girls do. Then we decorated our bare feet with a ribbon of liquid red *alta paint* and tied *ghungur (anklet with bells)*. We were set.

We put on the music and our performance started. People gathered around the courtyard and giggled with glee.

One of them was a patient of Dr. Kader whose face I recognized. Rebati, the *dhaki* (drum player). I had met him in the wayside cafe the day I tasted my first *monda*. I also remembered that I was kind of amused by his funny ways and strange disposition. I took him as a retarded person, a bit weird and slow.

Rebati started clapping with the beat and drumming a plain old wooden table. Someone gave him a pair of sticks and he started making amazing music banging on the metal pipes, wooden poles and stones.

Someone brought a *tabla* then a bongo. Rebati showed his mastery in percussion moving from one instrument to another and added incredible sounds from his mouth. He surprised me because I knew he had hard times with his tongue while talking and did stammer a lot to express himself.

He took out some marbles from his pocket, juggled them and dropped them at the precise second of the beat bringing a different dimension to this music. Then he entered the dance floor and joined us with fast footwork and went back to his percussion ensemble.

That evening he took us to a world of rhythm and sounds I did not know existed. He also showed me the meaning of off-beat and the power of silence.

When we were done Uncle Kader said, "Do you know what you were dancing to? Do you know the meaning of the song?"

"No, not quite. We guessed it is a folk song and we love the beat," I replied. Padma held her chin up, "It made us dance. So we danced." Dr. Kader and Babu exchanged glances and smiled.

"It's the words of common people. The farmers are saying— 'Hark! Watch out. Polish your scythe, brother. For the sake of lives and dignity. We are not going to give away all the harvest that we have reaped with our sweat and blood. Now we know your nature, oh landlords, how you patronize and line your own pocket with our labor. We are not going to give our precious fruits of labor anymore while dying in hunger."

This song was written after the Famine of 1942, a famine that was artificially created, and killed thousands of common people. It is a song from the *Krishok Bidroho* (Farmers' Revolution)." He explained.

I felt that I was at the farmers' side. This song struck a chord in me. I agreed with them.

Sipping cool lemonade served by a maid, I stretched out on the soft velvet sofa humming the tune.

15

THE ARTIST BOY

Budhon, nine or ten years of age, loved to paint. Stretching out his paper at one corner of the temple courtyard, he was creating an image of a home. A scene of a thatched roof cottage was taking place. Tall coconut trees stood behind this house with ripened fruits of chocolate color. A line of people with ebony dark skin was walking, scythes in their hands, three more behind a pair of cows. A woman in a striped red sari had a vessel on her head, and another, in yellow, next to her, placed the brass vessel at her hip. A small black and white goat with a tiny bell on its neck was sitting in front of the stick fence of the cottage. Bunches of carnelian orange flowers flocked at the front.

Budhon, absorbed in his artwork stretched out on the marble floor of the temple. At times he sprang up and walked back a few steps to examine his picture.

A passerby, fruits and flowers on her platter, chuckled at the child and climbed the steps. Fragrance of jasmine and marigold, sandalwood sticks and camphor filled the air. Rhythmic tinkles of brass bells with the hymns of a *kirtan* (Hindu religious song) floated from inside the temple:.

Horoye nomo, Krisna Jado bayo nomo, Jadobayo, Madhobayo, Keshobayo nomo,... Hori Horoye nomo.

At times Budhon's thin body swayed with that rhythm of the cymbals, but he did not go inside. He was too busy covering the blue sky with occasional red streaks of the setting sun. Today, for an auspicious celebration he wore an ivory-colored dhoti. At times he was using part of this cotton outfit for wiping off paints, sometimes using it as a blotting paper to give extra effect on his picture. Budhon got excited with this new experiment when an accident happened.

The red paint bowl toppled and smeared his tranquil picture with a bloody mess. Budhon shrieked. His piercing cry rattled the pious atmosphere. His mother came running and hurried to embrace him. She took him to her bosom and wiped off his tears, "Don't you cry, my child. It's no big deal. See, not all the paints are gone. You'll make a picture again. Don't you cry like that. What will people say?"

* * *

At that moment, there was another cacophony outside, at the other end of the temple. "Riot, riot, stay calm, everyone." A crowd of young men came running up the steps. "Ladies, mothers, and sisters, please be careful. Don't leave unescorted, stay inside the temple. Outside, it is dangerous."

I was there, and we soon came to know that a bunch of Muslims had attacked a neighboring Hindu colony. They attacked when the men were out at work and the women stayed home. The women did not have guns or knives or even know how to use them, but they defended themselves in a novel way. They poured hot, boiling water, the boiled starch liquid of the just-cooked rice from rooftops. The attackers did not anticipate this wild defense and ran away after a couple of gunshots.

At the other corner, there was also a swarm of people. They were using soft voices, hushing each other, exchanging nervous looks. It was my mother, supine on the floor. A lady was fanning her, another sprinkling water on her face. A *kabiraj* doctor was checking her pulse.

Two young men brought a rope bed. The doctor asked everyone to move away so that the patient could get fresh air. I felt nervous.

In a few minutes Ma opened her eyes, and with an embarrassed smile hurried to sit up checking her sari.
"You fainted for a short time. Everything will be okay, don't worry." Someone gave her some coconut water and the two young men insisted that she better lie down on the rope bed. The smell of medicine drowned the natural fragrance of the temple.

*   *   *

That evening in the faint light of a lantern in Dr. Kader's study, Dr. Kader and Rahmat were playing chess. Rahmat was a lead member of the local Islamic Party.

It was a muggy hot day. The windows and doors were wide open. Now and then a gust of breeze billowed the curtains, flying and scattering papers on the floor. The lantern flickered and ghastly shadows of the two men trembled on the wall.

Rahamat abruptly knocked Dr. Kader's bishop on the chessboard placing his ivory horse in its spot. With a flare of confidence he relaxed on the chair, "Now there is only one solution, one door open, Doctor, the surgical operation of India. Yes, I am quoting our leader, Jinnah Sahib, surgical operation on India. Punjab and Bengal must be parted, otherwise we, Muslims would have no place, no choice, no power."

Dr. Kader was quiet. Calmly he stepped a tiny black pawn and picked up Rahmat's queen. "Check mate!"

Rahmat, flabbergasted, hunched on the chess board. Biting the corner of his lip he stared at the board for a while. Then he touched various pieces and finally, "One second chance, please? Just this time?" he pleaded.

Dr. Kader stretched out in his armchair, placing both hands behind his head.

"What do we win, Rahmat, dividing India, cutting up our motherland?

All you see is 35 lakh Muslims and 30 lakh Hindus, the issue of majority and minority, power and position? Aren't you forgetting that we speak the same language, we hear the same music? We drown in the same flood, suffer in the same famine, die of the same disease. When there is an epidemic when I go to cure the patients, do I check if he is Muslim or Hindu?" The doctor was exhausted gusting away his suppressed emotion. He picked up a glass of water and drank all of it in one breath.

Then he continued slowly, "Rahmat, did you ever think of the fact that all the rice fields are at the west, all we have here is jute? But all the jute mills are in Kolkata? If there is a partition what will we eat? Can you fathom our destiny?"

Rahmat sat up straight. "You being a Muslim, you say that? You don't support us?"

"I see only one thing, that we are both ruled by the same British Raj." Dr. Kader sighed.

"What are you talking about? Yes, the British made us their servants, but can't you see what is happening in Kolkata? Aren't they beating us up there? Aren't they suppressing, killing us? After that bloody thing, you still feel we are brothers?" Rahmat scoffed.

The doctor took off his glasses and put them on the table. With a faint smile he looked at the board, "Rahmat, you were asking about a second chance in the game?"

Rahmat scratched his head and returned his queen on the board repositioning the other pieces as well. Then he touched different pieces trying different options for saving his *bibi (*queen*)*.

"You were talking about the surgical operation of India. Just remember it is not a game like this. Once the surgery starts there is no second chance, no going back. It is real life Rahmat. A river of blood will flow. Lots of people, lots of innocent people will die, lose homes and families. There will be terrible losses that we cannot even fathom today." Dr. Kader sighed.

*   *   *

"Jinnah Sahib is right. Divide India or destroy." Rahmat Ali's group shouted with placards in hands. "Inquilab Zindabad!" hollered the crowd.

The attack started in the Hindu colonies. Sticks and pick-axes, bombs and fire, they spared nothing. Looting, killing, raping went rampant. Pools of blood flowed, burnt huts and homes filled with ashes smeared the villages. Parvati was raped and converted to Parvin when her husband was killed in front of her. Anita, the grocer's wife jumped into the family well to save chastity.

Lakhan and his family packed up to move away. His widowed mother held their family *Tulsi mancha* (sacred basil tree) and nodded her head. "This is my soil, my home. Seven generations lived here. I am going nowhere." She sobbed.

Lakhan, irritated, tried to explain, "*Ahh* Ma! Can't you see our future here?"

"You are young, you have a future. You go. What future do I have left at this age? I'll be here. This precious little one will look after me. Won't you, child?" She caressed the chin of Ali, her Muslim neighbor's son. The ten-year-old boy looked at her, bewildered.

Finally, Lakhan filled up the bullock cart with bags, pots, and pans, and helped his children and wife to climb up. Then he brushed off his palms and touched his mother's feet, "I'll come and get you as soon as we find a place to settle."

* * *

In a few days, there was an arson in Goalpara, the colony of milkmen. Someone sprinkled kerosene at night on the haystacks and then threw a matchstick. Smoke simmered and smoldered and no one noticed. Early in the morning Budhon's mother filled the buckets with milk and went to distribute them to her customers like every day.

"Did you hear what happened?" a neighbor came running to her. The Goalpara is a sea of flame. It started this morning. What loud bursts and oh the smell of smoke and fire!" She covered her ears with both hands.

Budhon's widowed mother left her buckets of milk right there and ran as fast as she could until she reached the front of her house. It was engulfed in flames. One side had fallen down, the other part still standing was smeared in black soot. The villagers were throwing buckets of water to tame the flames.

"Budhon, my child, where are you?" she searched for him.

*　　　　*　　　　*

No, Budhon could not be saved.

When the neighbors draped his little body in a white sheet, resting him on a rope bed and picked up chanting *Hori Bol,* to do his last rite, his mother shrieked.

"Don't you take my boy away. He is all I am left with. Don't you take him away from me." She wailed.

A neighbor lady came forward and took her to her bosom. "Don't cry like that. Everything will be all right. God will take care of you. Now don't cry. What will people say?"

16

THE TEACHER

History was a boring subject until I met Bokul di, the history teacher, in my final year of school. Until then it was a list of dates and names of kings and queens, of a faraway land, of a distant past. I had to memorize them and then purge for the tests and then forget about them. Bokul di showed us that History could be stories of common people like us, of modern days that affect our lives.

Tall, with a slender build she had an absolute straight gait, almost like that of a ballerina. Her face looked young but somber. She hardly wore makeup or jewelry, or fancy clothes. Yet, she stood out distinctly in a pure spun cotton sari and a pair of gold glasses. The eyes behind those glasses had such kindness, such a strange power or depth it was impossible to lie to her. It drew out the honesty in you, straight.

And, she had a wonderful way of storytelling. We listened with pin-drop silence, mesmerized, where the characters fleshed out, acted alive, right in front of our eyes.

* * *

It was an early morning of March. The year was 1930. A man, about sixty years old was walking. He was wearing a piece of cotton loin cloth, showing off his thin shins and a hand-woven cotton shawl draped his upper bare body. There was still winter in the air, with crispy, chill nips. The eastern horizon had a splash of blush.

With a hunched gait, wooden sandals on his feet he moved on. His walking stick made rhythmic thuds.

Roosters crowed, a *kokil* (cuckoo) chirped joyous spring notes, *kuhu-kuhu-kuhu-koo-koo*. The old man paused, smiled, trying to find the bird, then continued his journey. The morning sun cast a long shadow on the ground, of his slim physique. He kept on walking, traveling forty-eight villages, two hundred and forty miles, for twenty-four days, non-stop, until he reached the seashore.

Villagers came bewildered, looked at him in awe. Then started to walk with him. Young and old, men and women, dignitaries and untouchables, from all walks of life, started following him until the procession became two miles long. Hundreds and thousands of people started joining in the march. Why?

This old man wanted to save his people, protest a tax, known as the Salt Tax. Salt is a daily necessity for all, and this salt is natural. British prevented common people to make sea salt, declared it illegal, and imposed a tax on it. This tax was as high as many people's two weeks' earning.

His name was Mohandas Karamchand Gandhi. His people called him Bapu ji, the Father of the Nation. Gandhi ji's weapon was nonviolence. Civil Disobedience.

On the fourteenth day they reached their destination, the village of Dandi. It was a similar early morning hour. The sun had just sprung up on the eastern horizon, happy, greeting, *'Shabash beta!'* (bravo, my child).

The white sand, on the seashore, dazzled in the morning light like diamond crystals. Gandhi ji picked up a handful, "This is nature's gift, a gift from the ocean. Why should we pay tax to the foreigners for this?" He shook his head. Then he opened his palm. The diamond crystals rained down on the ground.

British Raj showed him the consequence. They arrested 80,000 people. Police started beating them brutally. Many were killed. The nonviolent protest erupted at many places in India with the guidance of Gandhi ji's followers. In Peshawar, Gaffer Khan, a Muslim Pashto disciple of Gandhi led a similar demonstration. 230 innocent people were murdered in a bazaar where British Raj ordered open-fire to an unarmed crowd. They demonstrated nonviolence. One British Indian Army Soldier, Chandra Singh Garhwali was his name, refused to fire. His whole platoon was arrested. Many received life imprisonment.

Gandhi was not spared too. When they came to arrest him, Bapu ji held up his hands, with his clasped fist, filled with sand, announced, "With this, I am going to shake the foundation of the British Empire."

*   *   *

Sixteen years later, on a cold November afternoon, Bokul di met this personality.

"I became his disciple, and went to serve in his peace camp. Are you aware of what was happened in Noakhali?"

Mymensingh was a relatively peaceful place and we did not see or face much of the unrest but of course we were scared of what was happening in our neighborhood districts, just a couple of hundred miles away in the eastern part of Bengal.

On October 10, 1946, on a full-moon night when the Hindus were celebrating Kojagari Lakshmi Puja, the goddess of wealth and wellbeing, there was a horrible massacre in Noakhali. It started with an attack on a wealthy Hindu zaminder, in his own house, killing his whole family and guests, burning his house. The fight did not end there. Violence went rampant. More than five thousand Hindus were killed. They murdered husbands, brothers, and sons. Women were raped and abducted. Then they were converted to Islam. 50,000 Hindus were marooned under strict surveillance of the Muslims when the administration had no say. More than seventy thousand survivors were sheltered in temporary camps in neighboring districts like Comilla, Chandpur, and Agartala.

Gandhi came and tried to ease the tension creating peace camps in Noakhali and stayed there for the next four months. He always believed that the Hindus and Muslims were brothers, two sons of Mother India. But history did not quite agree.

Things got worse. The Congress Party finally decided to have the Partition of India in 1946. The peace camps were abandoned and the majority of the survivors migrated to West Bengal and Assam, which fell on the India side.

* * *

"The name of the village is Sri Rampur, in Noakhali district. The place resembles a jigsaw puzzle, of land masses and small islands surrounded by water. Rivers, canals, and ducts join the lands. The estuary is where the River Ganga meets Brahmaputra. Forty or fifty square miles of boggy, muddy land did not discourage its people. It is quite densely populated, mostly with Muslims. One in five people would be a Hindu." Bokul di continued.

"Small market places and tiny houses are connected with waterways and canals. A *majhi*, boatman in a dinghy or a skiff boat with oars would take you from one place to another. Sometimes you may have to take the narrow wooden or rope bridges that swing as you walk, your knees rattling in fearful tremor.

The huts are low and dark. Clay courtyards in front of each hut are cold and damp in the winter months. In such a humble place I met my guru, my teacher for the first time. Through a tiny crack a faint ray of light filtered in the room, showing off dust particles more than anything else. There, in that light, I saw him, Mahatma (the great soul).

He was sitting on the floor, on his heels, clutching his knees, resting his chin on bony knees, his gaze far away. *What was he thinking, or dreaming?*

'Bapu ji, I am Bokul, coming from Mymensingh, to get your blessings.' I touched his feet. Bapu ji put on his glasses, raised his face, then touched my head with a smile. 'Long live my daughter.'

* * *

Bapuji came here to calm down his people; as if he is the father, came to fix the fight between his two sons, as if it is partly his own fault. To do penance, he takes this expiatory journey, to visit all the forty-seven villages in Noakhali, walking one hundred and sixteen miles, one step at a time. He will go empty-handed, with no arms, no ammunition. He will be their guest. He will eat whatever they give him. He will beg them to stop this violence with love.

No, he does not want a procession or a big fuss, yet some of us follow him, thinking of his health and old age. Treading the muddy path, trampling thorny bushes, scratching himself, he proceeds humming a song written by his favorite poet:

> *If no one answers your call, you go alone*
> *if they all turn away, leave you in the dense forest, all alone,*
> *Trampling thorns under your bloody feet, you go alone.*
> *If no one shows you light, in that dark, stormy night*
> *Light up the flame in your heart*
> *Go you alone.*

Villagers crane their necks from windows, some come out of their huts and watch the drama of this naked *fakir*. Gandhi ji thinks maybe his mantra of nonviolence has started working, and he feels energetic in the beginning. Then he comes in front of a small cottage.

From far away he could see a bunch of children, seven or eight years of age, hear their cacophony. A *sheik* is teaching them in that *patshala*, village school. Seeing Gandhi he stands up, brushes off his dusty *lungi*, and strokes his beard.

Bapu ji scurries to greet him, rattling his walking stick. As if the grandfather has come to his children to embrace, he stretches his hands with a big toothless smile.

The *sheik* narrows his eyes. With knitted brows, he instructs the kids to go inside, as if someone has come to harm them. Gandhi folds his hands, greeting with a *namaskar*. The *sheik* eyes him top to bottom, then spits with a disgusting look slamming the door in front of Bapu ji's face. The children, bewildered, look at him from inside, holding the iron bars of the window, inside.

SHADOW BIRDS

Bapu ji's face turns pale. He takes off his glasses. He wipes them with the end of his shawl, then wipes his eyes. He walks again.

Gandhi ji realizes that each day the struggle gets harder. He could see festoons and notices hanging from tree-branches and poles that say, 'Leave. We want partition.'

He ignores them. Neglects them shoving away the feeling just like the thorns under his feet, around his path. Then he stumbles on to something; broken glass and human feces.

Gandhi ji stops, looks around and then breaks off a small branch. With it he brushes off. Using it as a sweeper he keeps on walking. He bends down to pick up the broken pieces of glass that cut his toe, sweeps it away, clears his path and starts humming... *if they leave you in the dense forest, trampling the thorns under your bloody feet you go alone.*

*   *   *

That evening after we return to the *ashram* cottage, Bapu ji busy picking the spear grasses from his clothes, his granddaughter, Manu massaged his feet with warm oil. In the faint light of clay lamps and lantern, his thin body casts a gigantic shadow on the wall.

'What are you thinking, Grandfather?' Manu asks.

Gandhi ji replied: 'You ladies are my strength. You are a big part of this fight for freedom; we must never forget, never ignore that. We must never forget the *dalits* too, the untouchables. I tell my wife that you have a reservation touching them because they clean our latrines, our waste? Which mom has ever been a mother without cleaning after her child, without wiping off her child's bottom? Purify your soul. You, my daughters, each of you teach this message. Show the world that love only has the power to solve this huge problem of violence and hatred.

It must be true, you know, otherwise, why did so many people come to see me when I went to England in 1931? I did not know those people. What message did they hear in my voice that the rail station in Paris overflowed with people from all over, so much so that they finally put me on top of the car?

I hold that picture in my mind often whenever I feel down. There must be an inherent truth in the message of nonviolence. There must be…'

The daylight was going down outside, fast. Gandhi ji came out of the hut cupping his palm on his forehead to see up in the sky a flock of birds was returning home."

*   *   *

The school bell bonged with loud clanks. Bokul di stood up from her chair. All the girls hurried to go out to lunch. I sat mesmerized, still in another world until Padma, my best friend, came and shook me. "Do you have money? Let's go see if the ice cream man has come."

17

THE BIRTH

Sound of conches woke me. It must be the celebration for the Independence Day. India is free! A new nation is born! Only a few days old. I jumped up and rolled the window shutters. No, there was nothing unusual outside. No bands, no bugles, no procession with a flag for the newborn country.

The morning sun was up but quite pale. The color of the sky was chalky white, rather colorless, there was really no color, only a wisp of grey. The day was muggy and hot already. The indigo skyline of the Sushong hills looked blurry, draped in a haze. Tall *supari* trees were standing still. Not a leaf moving, not a bud trembling with joy. Why? It was supposed to be a joyous time. We should have been tooting bagpipes and singing our new national anthem—*Jana gana mana adhinayak jaya he...*

Just then the conch blew again. *Pwooo, pwoooo, pwooo.* It was rather coming from inside the house, from the other end. Buri didi came running, "You have a baby brother, today! Come see him. Your mother gave birth to a son very early this morning, at dawn. Oh, it was a struggle. You know how your ma could not carry a child full term and this baby was quite early too. Before you came, she had two stillborn cases, you know. We were so scared, but both are well." Buri didi took a breath.

No, I knew none of that. Ma never told me. I thought Ma gained weight.

"Let's go!" I began to run down the long hall. We opened the door and Buri didi moved the curtain. I saw Ma holding a very tiny baby on her breast. She looked pale and exhausted, but she smiled and gestured me to come close. When I stood beside her bed, she drew me in and kissed my forehead, kissed my cheeks, my eyes. Warm tears from her eyes touched my lips. Ma had never done anything like this. "Want to hold him?" she asked me.

"First go wash your hands with soap and water." Dhuli didimoni smiled.

I ran to my room and took out my favorite blanket, my *nakashi kantha*. This would be the gift for my baby brother, I decided. A few minutes later as I laid it out smoothing the ends, Buri didi wrapped the baby in it and gave him to me like a little bundle. *How small, how very delicate he is. Yet, he has everything perfect. Ten tiny toes, and ten little fingers, a prominent nose like Babu, Ma's big eyes and perhaps the dark curls he inherited from me.* Then I remembered that I was really not his blood relative, how can he get my genes? Just then the baby curled his tiny finger to grip my pinky and I felt ashamed that a minute ago I was thinking he was not my brother.

"What are we going to call him?" I asked.

"Ashis (meaning blessing)." Ma replied

"Or Protik, meaning symbol. He is a symbol of freedom. We are free now," I said.

Kerchew, kerchew, the baby sneezed. "You are Sneezy, the dwarf, no Ashis, no Protik, baby." I laughed.

"What is that dwarf thing?" Buri didi asked with knitted eyebrows. I told her the story of Snow White and the Seven Dwarfs. "It is an English story," I said.

"How do you know English stories? It is not our language. Can you speak too like the sahibs and memsahibs?" Buri didi chuckled.

"I can read and I can speak too, little but it may not sound like them."

Buri didi was astonished. "Can you write too?"

"Some, not well though," I answered.

"Then, when you grow up, will you write our stories in English so that the sahib, mem-sahibs can read them too?" Her eyes shone.

I'd better go poke my friend, Padma, I thought. India is free, at least we must celebrate. I dressed up, took a platter full of sweets and headed towards my best friend's house.

Padma opened the door but her face was gloomy and somber. Not a smile, not a hug, not a greeting, she held the door and muttered, "What?"

I opened the door wide and entered; placed the platter on their table gave her a tight hug and kissed her cheeks.

She pushed me, "Did you come to say goodbye, that you are leaving too?"

This was my turn to exclaim "WHAT?" I took a breath, "No, I came to say that my baby brother was born this morning, very early this morning, and I brought some sweets to share the good news." I took one to her mouth.

My eyes fell on the newspapers that were scattered on the ground. In two-inch black bold letters it said, "The most horrendous massacre in history." A picture of a train to Lahore is on fire. People are oozing out from every direction; from doors and windows. The rooftop of the train is filled with people. Body parts of human beings are strewn on the platform, on the tracks—everywhere.

At the other corner of the paper, I saw a picture of a woman draped in a black burqa, her hands held up in the air, her face smeared with streaks of black. She is looking for her lost infant; it read. I bent down and turned the page. People in bullock carts, wagons are going. They are going somewhere. Migrating. Some on bare feet, some carrying old people in baskets on their heads, they are leaving their homeland. Refugees.

Padma looked straight into my eyes,

"Tell me, tell me the truth, that you are also leaving. Why are you hiding that from me?" Her eyes welled up.

"No silly, Why should we leave?" I smiled. "There is no such

SHADOW BIRDS

violence here, see it's quiet and peaceful. Mymensingh is not Lahore, my friend. We never think of leaving. Did you hear any gunshots and bombs? You might have heard the conch which was coming from our house because a son is born." I try to cheer her up.

"Do you know what Buri didi said? When a male child was born the custom of the zaminders was to blow the conches and *singua* (kind of bugle) to alert everyone as if there was a dacoit, an attack: 'Hey come to my house.' People would all gather at the zaminder's courtyard. Then the respected zaminder twirling his mustache would announce that there is good news. 'A son is born.' And his subjects would then dance and shout in merriment and demand a party. The zaminder would then throw a lavish party and distribute sweets and goodies to show his joy and generosity. But what if it were a girl? Then you kind of kept it quiet." I tried to make her laugh.

"So, are there many people in your courtyard now?" Padma asked with a raised eyebrow without a smile.

"Well, no, not really." I had to swallow. I had to admit that there should have been a more robust crowd for such an occasion in our family.

"Maybe they are on their way to reach the new land, Hindustan." Padma blurted.

I tried to shove this thought as far as I could and tried to be optimistic. But an unknown fear bobbed up. It was like trying to drown a balloon.

Refugee. That nasty word erupted in my quiet hours, messing up everything. The *sal* trees that lined the path leading to my favorite library, the cool water of the Glass Lake where I dipped my toes and played with the tadpoles, the blossoms of the *bokul* tree under which I spent many afternoons with my favorite books became more precious than ever. This was my home. Why on earth would I leave it for anything? Gypsy, our dog wagged her tail and licked me, and I cuddled her back.

*   *   *

Months passed and my little brother was growing fast. One day he showed his skill that he could turn all by himself. We were excited.

I saw that at the other corner of the room Buri didi and Dhuli didimoni were busy packing up. They were filling their trunks and suitcases with their belongings. They were going back to *Kashi,* Benaras, where they had come from, where it was believed that all destitute women found home.

One day Babu and I went to see them off at the train station. When the train came, we settled them and Buri didi found a seat near the window.

While we were waiting at the platform, a young man came and greeted Babu.

"Namaskar, do you know when the train for Kolkata will come?"

Babu replied that it was scheduled to come within a few minutes at the opposite platform. The young man thanked him and requested if we could keep an eye on their luggage as he had to bring his invalid father.

An old man came very slowly walking with an ambulatory stick, and plopped on the metal trunk.

I looked through the train window at Buri didi and found a strange expression on her face. In her wide eyes there was a look of disbelief and discovery. Her jaw dropped, she was mesmerized. When she collected herself she gestured me to come close.

"What did the young man tell your father?"

I told her that he was the son of some doctor named Salil Bose, and they were waiting for the train to Kolkata.

Buri didi whispered, "It's him. It's him. That young man looked just like his father at that age. That is when I met him, twenty-three years ago. Baba Biswanath had heard my prayer, see! Remember one day I prayed to Baba that may I be able to see him one more time in my life? He heard my prayer!"

I nodded. Standing on tiptoe to reach her hand through the train window, with tears rolling down my cheeks I assured, "Yes, he answered your prayer."

The train jerked and slowly started moving, leaving the platform.

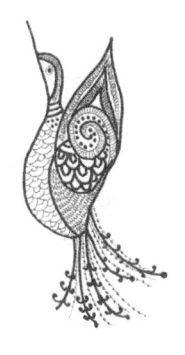

18

THE RECOVERY ACT

One day Jasimuddin came to Babu in the garden.

"Sir, do you know something called umm, umm, the Recovery Act?" Babu brushed the soil off his palms and looked into Jasim's face.

"Yes, something about recovering abducted women affected during the riot, I guess. I am not very clear, though Jasim, but I can find that out for you." He smiled and went back to his digging. Jasim bowed his head, a gesture showing thanks.

Jasim added, "I have some relatives in my house, Sir, my cousin, Goffur and his wife. She was a Hindu before and she suggested to my cousin that he seek help from you. She said that she knew you somehow and she thinks you may help."

"Strange! Where do they come from?" Babu went back to digging a bigger hole with his trowel.

"Noakhali, Sir. They desperately want to meet you. They are in great danger and came to me… um… kind of escaping. She says you can help." Jasim sounded anxious. It was decided that Jasim would bring them the next day to visit us. In the meantime he gave a glimpse of the background story.

SHADOW BIRDS

It was a normal day, Sati, Goffur's wife was busy with her daily chores inside the house that afternoon when their wooden entrance door shook. She heard banging, someone rattling, clanking the metal chain. A loud voice bellowed through a microphone.

"This is to notify that according to the Recovery and Restoration Act of India and Pakistan that if there is a woman in your custody who was abducted or has changed religion, you must inform the state immediately. Within two weeks you are to notify the state and register at the local police depot. It is the law. You must register within two weeks at the local office. Again, it is the law. This is to notify…"

Sati did not open the door. She touched her bosom with a sigh of relief that today the front door was locked unlike most days. Usually, she kept it open for the neighbors. Sati did not open it now but through the little crack she could see a military officer in a tan uniform with a pistol hanging from his belt. The man then got into his jeep and in a swirling cloud of dust, the vehicle left.

Looking down, she found a yellow piece of paper on the ground which had been slipped under the door. Sati picked it up and saw that it was addressed to the men of India and Pakistan. Both countries had come to an agreement to implement the Recovery and Restoration Act for abducted women. Sati knew how to read and she carefully went through each word. It said—any abducted person who is found to be living with or under the control of any individual or family will be recovered and given back to the country she originally belonged to. If this female is a Hindu, she shall go back to India. If she is a Muslim, she must return to Pakistan. It also said, if a child is born within the period of 1st March 1947 to 1st January 1949, that child will be considered a citizen of the country where he was born. The child will remain with the father.

Sati then read under the words 'Power of the Police' in bold letters, that the police would have full authority to enter, search, and take into custody any person he believes has been abducted. He would not need a warrant to do so. The note also asked citizens to comply with this law and help the police officers to find and locate any such victims in their neighborhood. It is the law, it reminded again in big letters at the bottom.

Sati felt dizzy as if the whole courtyard was swirling in front of her. She held the bamboo pole and sat down taking a deep breath. She thanked God one more time that today the front door was locked. Then she hurried to check her little son who was sleeping peacefully. Sati drew the blanket over him and kissed his forehead.

Tears gushed and turned into uncontrollable sobs. When her husband, Goffur Miya returned home, the sun was down at the horizon. He called her name looking for her in all familiar places. Today he had come through the back door; now he saw that the front door was locked from inside. His wife should be inside somewhere. He found her, sitting on the step holding the pole.

"There you are! What happened, any bad news?"

Sati handed him the yellow note though she knew it was useless. Goffur was illiterate. He looked blank as Sati tried to explain it between sobs.

"We must get out of here, as soon as possible." She wailed.

Goffur embraced her and kissed her forehead.

"Arreh baba, no one will take you away. You are my *bibi* (wife), mother of my son." Sati rested her face on his chest, she could hear the thumping of his heart.

"Doesn't matter, Miya, the law is law. You must notify them within two weeks. Everybody here knows who I am, how I became your wife converting from Hindu Sati. How once I did worship my goddess Lakshmi. The Police Office does have the power to take me."

Then she mumbled, "Where were those Police Officers when the riot broke out, when the whole village was on fire? What were those Police Officers doing then? Never mind, didn't you say that you have a cousin in Mymensingh who works for a Hindu zaminder family? Maybe they can help us. Somehow I have a gut feeling that will be the best thing for us to do now. Let's get out of here."

Goffur nodded. Sati raised her face and looked into Goffur's eyes. "At least they may know some way we can appeal, or ask for an exemption. We need someone who knows the laws." Goffur was impressed that his bibi, though a woman, understood these things better than he did. Next day, early in the morning, Sati, Goffur and their little boy set for Mymensingh.

The tall *sal* trees along the river bank made a dark silhouette. The river lay flat like a silver sari, the sun rising on it like a vermillion dot. Sati remembered this place. *Nijhum Dweep* (tranquil island) they called it. She had come here so many times before with her family, in such early hours to take a dip, worshipping the Sun God with salutation mantras. She could hear her father-in law's voice in her head reciting.

Om Jaba kusum sankasan, I salute you oh Sun God for protecting us from death and darkness. You created us, for you we sustain, because of you I am… peace, peace, peace… Om Shanti, Om Shanti, Om Shanti, he had translated the meaning to her.

Today, she kept it all to herself. The boatman was ready even at this dawn hour. Sati remembered his face. Last time he refused them because he was forbidden to take any Hindu passengers. It was the same boatman who had served her family so many times before, since her childhood. Today he gave her a big smile, his typical one-tooth smile and took them aboard. From there the train station was not far.

*   *   *

When Jasim brought them to our house Babu was ready, but he also knew that Sati might feel uncomfortable in front of an unknown man. So he decided to sit in the adjoining veranda while Ma and I entertained Sati inside. Ma and I were in the room and Jasim took my brother Ashis and the little guest boy, Bubai to the garden to play. Goffur came and sat beside Babu.

Sati entered. A tall, slender woman, a few years older than me. In the beginning she covered part of her face with her sari. When she saw it was just us women, she uncovered her veil.

She looked around the room and went close to a picture that was hanging on the wall. It was a picture of *Balakrisna*, Krishna as a baby, stealing cheese balls from an earthen pot. Sati smiled and a cute dimple formed on her left cheek.

"What's your name?" Ma asked.

"Saburah." She replied with downcast eyes. Then she raised her chin.

"But I was Sati, Sati Bala," Her voice croaked. Ma offered her a glass of water. She took it. After a while she took a long breath and said, "I must be brave to tell you my story, the whole story, and I pray that you can do something." The woman stared at the ground for a while. Silent. Then wiped her tears and took a deep breath.

"It was the auspicious night of *Kojagari Lakshmi Puja* in Noakhali, where we lived. Every year on that special night our zaminder babu used to invite the whole village to his house. Like every year, we went there on that full moon night of October 1946. But this time the happy occasion turned into a horrible massacre.

Gunshots and rattling sticks drowned the prayer hymns and the *kirtan* (Hindu religious songs). People ran in all directions tripping over plates of sweets and flowers. A riot broke out immediately. The zaminder Ray Bahadur was attacked and killed brutally. Not a single member of his family was spared. One of his sons tried to protest and fight back. He was tied and burned alive. They poured kerosene on their house and set it on fire." Sati paused, her eyes were wet.

I had read and heard about the Noakhali massacre before. Gandhi ji had gone there to calm the people and was unsuccessful. Hearing it from someone who had experienced it firsthand was a different experience.

"We ran, ran and ran until we came to our own home. On our way we saw that our neighboring village was in flame. It was the village of the fishermen, and we thought we were spared."

Sati continued, "My father-in-law was a respected Brahmin headmaster of the school in our village. One day our house was also attacked, but some of the boys were my father-in-law's students. They requested that he be spared and they spared us.

In a short while the scenario changed. We found that the Hindu minorities had no way to escape. Noakhali is a place that has more waterways than land roads. We needed to cross those canals and ducts, but we were refused. They were blocked by Muslim forces. The boatmen were instructed not to serve Hindu passengers. The same people who were our neighbors the other day, were forced to become unfriendly aliens.

One day our nephew, Sudip, came running. Between his gasps and panting he told us about a lecture being given by a leader of the Muslim League. He quoted from the Quran that all idolators who worship statues and dolls are *kafir*. There is only one Allah, and every Muslim must protect that. Non believers must be converted or finished.

This lecture was on the same day of the Kojagari Lakshmi Puja, October 10, 1946. It energized the mob. They burned the Hindu villages. Sudip said, 'Sometimes they were not even the local Muslim people, but real soldiers. They were looting, killing and raping women. They were gang raping women in front of their husbands, fathers and brothers. Then they tattooed and imprinted their names and the date of the rape on women's body parts. They killed the men in front of the women. They cut off the raped woman's breasts and private parts, while no one did anything. Zaminder Ray Bahadur had asked for police help, which they blatantly denied. And now the Zaminder Ray Bahadur was killed too.'

My brother-in-law, Sudip's father added, 'Here we are a terrible minority. There is no law. We have no protection. What are we going to do?'"

At this point Sati stopped and shook her head. She hid her face behind her knees, sitting in a crouched position on the floor, hugging her knees, rocking herself, trying to control her sobbing. After a few minutes she forced herself to look up.

With intermittent sniffs she continued in a somber voice, "I came to know that we, women should jump in the well to save our chastity, to respect our sacred family name. It was better to kill yourself than let yourself be raped, when your father or husband could not protect you. My husband, his brothers and all the men agreed that yes, that was the noble way to do it.

Next morning the men made us drink gulps of *siddhi* after our prayer. I felt dizzy and confused. I found myself joining the procession towards the well with the other Hindu women. I took off my jewelry, my wedding ring and bangles, the fourteen rupees that I had saved and threw them on a communal shawl that was collecting every woman's precious belongings. It would be tied and thrown in the well first ceremoniously, then we would jump one by one. That was the plan.

We all marched, crying and scared. We tried to hide that feeling and be brave, some of us were chanting something that I did not understand. I did not care.

Suddenly, I got stuck. A bushy thorn grabbed my petticoat. I fell. My ankle got twisted. I sat down with an enormous pain. Women, like crazy people passed me, oblivious of my condition. They did not hear my crying. No one stopped for me. They went on like intoxicated ghosts, crying some mantra. They just passed me.

I crawled and dragged myself under a tree where I lost consciousness. When I woke, the sun had gone down. A big orange moon shone behind a tree. A barn owl hooted- who who who! I stared at it.

You did not let me die, at least not today, not yet. Why? Why did you do that, goddess Mother Lakshmi? I gazed at the moon for a long time stretched out under that tree. Then I heard a deep voice inside me. It whispered, I don't want to die. Not yet.

I stood up and dragged myself home. The house was empty. No one lit the lamps today. I arranged to do it in the dark. My husband came. he was shocked to see me. It was as if he had seen a ghost. 'What happened? Were you too scared to jump?' he mocked at me.

He did not notice but my niece, Kusum, fourteen years old, came running and hugged me. 'Kakima (aunty), I could not do it either. What happened to your leg?' She noticed my swollen ankle and brought some turmeric and lime and covered it with a cloth. She embraced me tight, 'Kakima, I could not die either.'

My husband said, 'As long as I am alive I'll not let you face all that they are doing to our women. I have my *bonduk* (gun).'

Here is a little story about that gun."

"Gun!" Ma exclaimed.

Sati shook her head and this time a faint smile rose and fell deepening her dimple. The tiny nose stud on her sharp features shimmered. It seemed like she had become shy and couldn't speak.

"What happened then, tell us that little story, Sati." Ma was impatient.

Sati nodded, "Yes, I promised to tell you everything, the whole story. When we were about to get married, my father had asked if there were any dowry demand or wish.

My father-in-law replied, 'Your daughter in our house will have what we have. There is no demand from my part, give whatever you wish to your daughter. But yes, talking about wish, my son does have a wish. A gun! to protect his beautiful bride, I guess,' he laughed.

He said jokingly, but my father presented a gun to my husband on our wedding. And my husband was very proud of that possession."

Sati paused with a faraway gaze, then started, "After the march, one night my husband decided that the men should all kill themselves before submitting to the Muslim force. His clan agreed. Bang, bang it went non stop.I tried to protest. Bang! I was hit too.

When I came to my senses I found the bodies of my husband, his two brothers, Sudip, his innocent sister, Kusum all lying flat, bloody. Dead.

The only person they forgot was my father-in-law, the old schoolmaster. Terribly sick he had stayed in his room. He was depressed and hardly talked during these days. I went to him. He sat up in bed and held out his arms. I hugged him and we held each other, drenched in tears.

This time when the looters came they kicked our statues of gods, framed goddesses from our praying alter. They took whatever they thought was valuable and then tied our hands. We made no fuss. They took us in a van to a big hall where we sat with all the low caste poor people who usually saluted us. That day we were all sitting on the floor, in the same line.

A man in a tan uniform handed us each a yellow paper, and another brought some ink to take thumbprints. The leader in a white *salwaar-kurta* and a *fez tupi* on his crown announced that our lives were saved, but no idol worshipping would be tolerated anymore. We were to believe in the Islam religion from now on.

My father-in-law, a devoted religious Brahmin, threw off his *paita* (the sacred thread that distinguished him as a Brahmin), and put on the *fez tupi*. The educated headmaster of the village didn't even bother to look at the yellow paper. He held out his right thumb like an illiterate, confirming that he was giving away his religion willingly and converting to a Muslim; and no one had pressured him to do that. That is what the yellow paper said. I had read it.

I broke my conch bangles, the sign of a Hindu married woman and wiped off my *sindur* dot from my forehead.

The Mullah converted all of us at the same time in a big group and told us how we should lead our daily lives with Islamic prayers and rituals. Then he announced that now the Hindu women were to be taken and given to various Muslim men as their wives or concubines so that the women were protected. I looked back. My father-in-law looked blank. We have never seen each other since then.

I was given to Goffur Miya. He had lost his wife the winter before. Goffur Miya became my new husband. I became his new wife Saburah.

Goffur has never been cruel to me. Rather, he is gentle. He works hard. I have learned how to help him in the field. I am learning many things I did not need to know before. There is a roof over our head, some food at the end of the day. And the most important thing, he gave me Bubai, our loving son. I am thankful to God.

Now this new rule says that they are recovering us. How? I have to leave this life, my son, my husband, and go to an unknown land where I knew no one? I have no family in India. Who is going to protect me? What family are they talking about? Why do they make such a cruel law in the name of recovery?"

Sati broke into uncontrollable sobs. Ma held her, trying to console.

I was numb. My cheeks felt warm, my earlobes burning, at the same time I felt goosebumps and started shaking with an intense emotion. Was it anger, the insult on behalf of all women I felt ? or the helplessness? I don't know.

*   *   *

No, my father could not show any law that could have them excused. There were no ways they could be exempted, other than just not being there. We came to know that similar things had happened at the other end, in Punjab too, where Muslim women were abused. Both the countries, India and Pakistan, had created this new law, Recovery and Restoration Act of 1949, for the abducted women.

It was strange that both nations differed in everything and therefore had to cut their motherland into two pieces, created a partition in the name of freedom, yet they agreed to implement this cruel law. They never realized what price women had to pay in this struggle for freedom.

No, Babu could not find a solution for Sati, but he invited them to stay with us, as long as they wished. So, they stayed in our guest quarter which was empty now since Buri didi and Dhuli didimoni had left.

The two little boys, Ashis, my brother and Bubai became friends and played in our garden.

19

ONLY ONE FAULT

"The girl had one fault. Only one fault." Dr. Kader murmured as he was taking off his hospital coat. He had just come home after a long day at the hospital.

Padma and I both looked up from our board game at his face when Dr. Kader turned to us, "Do you know a girl named Ashmani? Seemed like she went to your school."

"Why of course, she is our classmate, but she's been absent for quite a while. She is an excellent dancer. Oh Papa, if you had only seen her dance! Actually, she was chosen for the Srimati's role in the beginning, but her family objected her to take part… It was Saraswati puja, a Hindu thing you know, and they are Musselman." Padma stood up in excitement.

I remembered her too. The last time I saw her was that event night after the dance show. But I did not say anything. I wanted to keep that feeling to myself.

Dr. Kader shook his head and slowly dragged himself to the washroom. He looked exhausted and tired today. His face was somber and sad and we did not dare to ask anymore.

In a few days, Ashmani became a hot topic in school. Various stories, lots of rumors and gossips revolved around this character.

From all these sources, different neighbors' stories, school friends', Padma's and finally Dr. Kader's comment I collected her story.

Asmani was born in a Muslim farmer's family. When she was born her mother looked at her face and thought she was a fairy, and named her Ashmani, heavenly. Ashmani's mother wanted to give the daughter all that she had longed in her life and was deprived of. The mother sold her only pair of gold bangles so that Ashmani could go to a good school. When Ashmani grew older, mother saw promises of a dancer in her movement and slender figure. She worked extra hard in the field to make more money and pawned whatever valuable jewelry she possessed so that Ashmani could learn dancing from the best teacher. This made the fellow villagers raise their eyebrows.

Ashmani was no heavenly fairy in reality. She was just like any sixteen-year-old girl with the desire to be loved, and have fun. In the mornings when the fishermen's daughters tugged the wide nets and cleaned fish, the farmers' wives toiled in the rice fields, their bare feet muddy, sweat beading their forehead, Ashmani got ready for school. Her just-washed hair cascaded down her shapely back, her copper complexion shimmering in the morning sun. One day Ashmani was taking a shortcut to school through the narrow path beside the broken masjid. Mullah sahib was brushing his teeth with a long neem stick. His brows knitted.

"Ey Ashmani, can't you keep your head covered? Didn't your family teach you any modesty?"

Ashmani swayed away the unruly strand of hair from her face, "See, both my hands are tied", she giggled holding her hands up in the air, one showing a stack of books, the other a grocery bag. The cool spring breeze teased the lock on her forehead. A *kokil* joyfully sang *kuhu kuhu koo*.

Mullah sahib spat, disgusted at the audacity of the girl.

Ashmani's heart was full of glee that morning, beaming, like the sun-glistened waves of Rupsa river. She could not forget the look that she had seen yesterday on Torit's eyes. She played that over and over in her mind trying to fathom what it meant. Torit was the grocer's son.

Torit's father was an established businessman, quite well-liked. He kept high-end products in his store catering to the affluent ones as well as allowed credit to the poor people letting them pay later. He loaned people cash with interest, but he was the person to whom poor people could go to when they were desperate. Some said that he even played the role of a pawnbroker and Ashmani's mother did get some help from him.

Usually in the afternoons when he took a nap after lunch the son took charge of the grocery store. And this was usually when Ashmani visited after school to pick up their daily shopping items. Ashmani realized that when her mother forgot an item and sent her to the store one more time with apologies, she loved it. She wished such forgetfulness happened more.

One day after she came home, unloading the groceries, she found a bar of chocolate. She was quite surprised. She did not pay for it, nor could they afford such extravagance. Ashmani ran to break it and share with her little sister. Then she paused. She decided to hide the chocolate bar high up on a shelf behind other boxes. Torit's look flashed like a lightning in her memory. Her own reflection in the mirror caught her eyes. Ashmani glimpsed at that face, checked her hair and lips and smiled back. *Does Torit like me?* She looked around. No, no one had noticed.

Ashmani toyed with that feeling. At one time it filled her whole existence as if she were a sitar whose strings were played in harmonious joy. At other times it scared her. An eerie feeling, as if she was jumping from a high cliff to a dark pit. She felt dizzy. A shiver went through her entire body.

The other day she was on her way back from the store when it started raining. In the beginning it was just drizzling. Within a short time dark clouds gathered all over and a storm started. Thunder bolted, lightning sparked which she could see through the glass windows of the store.

"Come, I'll take you home. How can you walk home alone in such weather? Just wait here for me." Torit remarked pulling down the metal shutters with loud clanks.

He helped her climb the horse carriage and shut the door. Torit pulled the covers to prevent the rain sleet. Sitting beside Torit in that tonga, just the two of them, Ashmani felt electric shocks in her body. Butterflies fluttered inside her belly. She had no idea of such physical sensations before this. It was strange and scary both.

Torit held her hand suddenly.

"Ashmani, I wanted to tell something. I had been trying to articulate it from quite a while, but could not find the right words, the right time. All that I feel for you. When I am awake, I wait eagerly to meet you. I wonder when I can see you, when you will come. The days when you don't come, I feel them all wasted. When I am asleep, you come in my dreams. I realize that I can't live without you. I have given myself to you, not knowingly, not consciously. I don't know when it happened, how it happened, but it has happened. This is the truth."

Ashmani was shocked. Even though she felt the same way, she did not disclose it. Instead, she pulled her palm away.

"Torit, this is not right. This dream of yours has no meaning, no result. You are Hindu, we are Muslim. Our relationship cannot survive. No one will accept it. You must forget all that you have said to me and promise that you will never think like this. Promise me, otherwise, I will never come to you again. Such words are sinful!" Ashmani covered her ears with her hands. The glass bangles on her arms slid jingling away.

Torit looked at them and smiled. Ashmani noticed that too through the sudden lighting. Thunder clapped. When the loud shock disappeared, Torit brought his face close to her ears and whispered,

"Darling Ashmani, my sweet girl, I think I know you more than you know yourself. Your emotions were captured long ago when you blushed every time you saw me. You could not hide that, dear friend. I love you, and you love me too, which you fail to hide!"

"Torit, your family, my family, this whole village, our town, no one will accept such a marriage, don't you understand that?"

"Then we will elope. I will run away with my beautiful bride." Torit held her hands in his.

"Where will you escape Torit?"

"We will go far away, in another land, where no one knows us. We will start fresh. No one will judge us for our difference in religion. Our love will be our only testimony, our only identity. We will escape there, Ashmani. You and I, agree?" Torit squeezed her palm.

"No Torit, I can't let that happen. I believe in Allah. I am scared to go against my religion. This is my sin. Please, don't you ever think of me like that." Ashmani took her palm away.

The rain was torrential. The driver shouted, "Sir, the horses cannot run in this weather. Shall we take a break under the tree for safety?" As soon as the carriage stopped, Ashmani rushed, climbed down and ran into that dark stormy night.

Yet, like two poles of a magnet, they came close frequently. They both looked forward for accidental visits, though Ashmani had stopped going to the store in the afternoons where Torit was there alone. But she bumped into him on her way back from school, at the bank of Rupsha river where she often went in need of solitude.

Each such visit ended up with a fight. Ashmani's warning that it would be her last visit failed hopelessly, since they could not stay away from each other for long.

One day Torit announced that he was going away, leaving this place forever. His father was thinking of opening another branch in Krishnanagar, couple of hundred miles west. Would Ashmani join him?

Ashmani shook her head. No, she did not want to leave everybody, her beloved village, her religion to escape with Torit. She was clear.

"If you make my life miserable like this, then I have no choice but..."

"But what? But what Ashmani?" Torit cried out.

"Other that killing myself. Take poison and die. Commit suicide." She held her chin up and looked straight into his eyes.

"Take poison? Where would you get that, Ashmani?"

"Why, dear Torit, don't you know we are farmer people? We need to keep the rodents away. Don't forget that I have access to that. In fact, I had to scatter those rat poison every now and then when the pests are rampant."

"Ashmani, never ever think in that line. Didn't you say that you believe in Allah? I think your religion says it is sinful to hurt someone who has done no evil to you. It is wrong to crush someone's soul and heart. You have done that to me, while all I did was... I only loved you. But killing one's self, committing suicide is unforgivable. They have no place in heaven. Did you ever think of that?" Torit warned.

Then he sighed, "In case you change your mind I will be waiting at the river bank and take the boat at dawn tomorrow. You have the rest of the day and the whole night to think." He stood up and left.

That night Ashmani could not sleep. Her eyes were burning. Every time her tired eyelids closed she felt as if someone had just shaken her and she was falling down in a dark hollow pit. Ashmani woke herself and the same thought would swirl in her head, over and over. She felt scared, scared to face the next day. In a few hours the morning sun would rise. She was afraid and hid her face in the pillow.

A few minutes later she saw Bonu, her little sister was asleep beside her. Ashmani moved her thin limb that was embracing her. Mother too, was breathing heavily, in deep sleep. And her father's rhythmic snoring guaranteed his peaceful deep slumber after a hard day.

Ashmani stood up, tightened her sari. In quiet tiptoes she went to the door and unlatched the chain. She opened and closed it without a sound. Outside was still dark, only a sliver of moon.

Ashmani ran. Ran as fast as she could until she reached the bank of the Rupsha river. Torit was standing right under the *bokul* tree. Ashmani thrust herself onto this chest. Torit held her tight.

"I knew you would come." He kissed her forehead, her cheeks, her lips.

"Come, hold my hand, the boat is right there. Be careful." Torit stretched his hand. Ashmani shook her head.

"No Torit, I can't go with you. I just came to say goodbye to you. To tell you, that I didn't mean to ever hurt you. Believe me, I am hurt too, for all that has happened. I was ignorant. I didn't know better. Forgive me and forget me please, and be happy in your life. Please! Promise you have forgiven?" This time Ashmani grabbed his hands for the first time and held them in hers.

Torit pulled them away. Then he put his right hand in his pocket and took out something wrapped in a handkerchief and gave it to her. Ashmani opened it and found a tiny gold locket in a chain.

"I bought it for you, thinking of you, a small wedding present. Can't give it to anyone else that was meant for you. Be happy whoever you marry." Slowly he walked down the slope and stepped on the boat unfurling the rope.

A swarm of people were standing in a half circle, enjoying this fateful drama. The respected Mullah sahib stepped forward and exclaimed, "Did you see the nerve of this girl? I knew she was spoilt long time ago, when she wandered around with a book in her hand, swaying her hips, head uncovered, sleeking her hair immodestly. I knew it. I warned her. Did she care? And look at the family… Couldn't they teach her better manners?" Mullah sahib brushed his beard with his fingers.

Someone got him a rope cot to rest. He plopped and said,

"I did not become a Mullah just like that. What does the holy book say? It says: women, believer of Allah, keep your head covered, your hair, your ears, neck, bosom; your ornaments, keep them covered. Be modest. Don't seduce men. Don't start the flame. Right, folks? Right, my brothers? If you have doubt, go check Surah-an-nur, ayah 31. Go check it, if I am wrong. I did not become a Mullah for nothing just like that!" he jerked his head and brushed his beard.

All the people nodded, agreeing, "Of course, of course, *huzur*!"

The fisherman's wife elaborated how shocked she felt to see the two in a tight embrace, kissing each other.

"Does the girl have no fear, no shame?"

Another woman replied, "They say a little learning is a terrible thing. When a farmer's child starts going to school like the women of zaminder families, I knew the poor thing will soon be in trouble."

Even Mahim, the converted sweet-maker added, "When women make such mistakes, the whole family pays for that." Hossain, his brother-in-law smiled though and teased him, "But Mahim, are you any worse off being a Musselman now?"

"No, no, I am not saying that. I am happy to be one of you. I'll do anything for that." Mahim managed. The Mullah started:

"This needs to be addressed. That girl needs to learn consequences. If her family fails, we as a community have the right and the responsibility for that, so that it does not happen again. Right, my brothers? Everyone must learn from such mistakes. Besides, it is not only the girl, her man should also pay his share. Well, he escaped. But his father still has his business. You must all go and charge him for his son's wrongdoing. Demand for a thousand rupees, not a paisa less! Never trust a non-believer, *kafir*." He spat.

Then he continued, "For now we must charge Kissan, the girl's father to pay one hundred rupees for failing as a father, he should have known better, right?" he nodded to the crowd.

"Yes, huzur." The crowd responded.

Ashmani's father came forward, both hands clasped, praying:

"*Huzur*, I admit that I failed to raise my daughter properly, but I am a poor farmer. Where would I get that kind of money? Mercy upon me sir, beat as much as you want, punish the unlucky girl, punish her for her wrongdoing. I was busy in the field, under the hot sun to provide for them, to bring food to the table, sir. I did not have that time sir. I failed to see what was going on. Please forgive me."

"Well then, your daughter should pay for that. Instead of one hundred slashes let's do another hundred more. Would that do, my brothers, what do you think"? The Mullah turned his head asking the crowd.

"Whatever you order sir, You are our master," they admitted.

"Well then one of you will have to take the responsibility of the job, disciplining, I mean." Mullah sahib ordered.

Aziz the *lathial* was chosen. He came forward. A leather belt was handed to him, some British sahib's thrown away belt, perhaps.

The girl was brought tied with ropes that the villagers used for tying their unruly cattle and fastened it around the trunk of the tree. As the leather belt lashed in the air *sh sh,* Aziz's bulging biceps glistened with vigor and sweat. His teeth clenched ferocious under thick dark mustache.

The men kept on counting ninety-eight, ninety-nine, one hundred.

Women covered their mouths muttering *chi chi*, what a shame.

No one said a thing except Ashmani's little sister, eight years old, Bonu. The child jumped around screaming "Why are you doing that? Stop. Look she is bleeding. Stop. Stop. STOP."

She cried holding both her ears until someone dragged her out of the scene.

"This is called consequences, punishment, you understand!" a man barked.

Ashmani stood still, her eyes focused far away as if she was a statue made of copper, not flesh and blood. At one time it ended. They untangled the rope and left one by one. Ashmani fell unconscious.

When her senses came back she found herself all alone under that same *bokul* tree where she had her first kiss this morning. The rising sun she was so scared to face last night was going away now, setting under the Rupsha river, drowning in disgrace to witness all these and able to do nothing. Night appeared blue-black, bruised in shame.

When Ashmani reached home, all was quiet. There was no cooking fire today, Her father and mother turned their faces away pretending to be asleep. Only, little Bonu held her hand, brushing her wounds. Then at one time she also fell asleep. The clay lamp flickered and went out.

Ashmani got used to that darkness. She felt her stomach was growling, her mouth felt dry. All day long she had not a drop of water, not a bite to eat. She raised herself, dragging to the kitchen. She lit a candle, took out the chocolate bar and then the packet of rat poison. She took a bite of the chocolate bar, oh so heavenly. Then she took the rat poison and drank all the water from the clay jug.

"*Astaghfirullah*! Forgive me Allah! Forgive me." She closed her eyes.

Next morning when she was brought to the hospital, Ashmani was gone. The villagers asked Dr. Kader to sign her death certificate.

"She was a farmer's daughter but went to Bidyamoyee school. Her name was Ashmani, but she'd have no room in heaven, we suppose!" laughed one of the villagers.

SHADOW BIRDS

"A tiny gold locket was discovered in the crease of her breast, doctor, the dead body, I mean," exclaimed another.

Rahmat, Mahim, and Aziz with a crowd of villagers joined in, "Good, that will fix the roof of the broken Masjid."

*   *   *

Ashmani's spirit remained with me forever. It still haunts me, in my quiet hours, dancing like a firefly, a shadow bird. I so wish to let it free, let it fly to heaven.

20

SKY LAMP

Ashmani's death shook me. Often she wandered in my thoughts. While I tried focusing on Geometry, my mind meandered somewhere else. I saw Ashmani. She'd dance right in front of my desk; swirled round and round her canary yellow *ghagra* with burnt sienna polka dots. The tiny embroidered mirrors from her skirt reflected circles of light, spinning around, making me dizzy. Her body oscillated in *chakras* and *tatkars* and stopped at precise beats. She'd stretch her mehendi painted palm to me, with a *selam*, touching her forehead, like a Mughal *baiji* court dancer, expecting me to applaud *kya bath, kya bath*.

It was all an illusion.

I tried to concentrate again. My tests were not too far away. This Matriculation examination would determine my future. I tried to remind myself. But my mind drifted. I could not help eavesdropping Ma and Sati's conversation from the other room.

"Do you know the grocery store, that Ma Tara store, is closed now, closed forever?" Sati announced.

"Really? Why? It was the biggest one in town. He was doing very well, I suppose. Just closed the store like that?" Ma was surprised.

"What else could he do, Didi? All that scandal with his son and that Muslim girl... after all he is a Hindu, *na?* The neighborhood boys will tear him to pieces. *Chhire khabe je!"* Sati explained.

"That girl messed it all up. What was she thinking? A marriage between Hindu and Musselman? I'd be upset too if I find my son bringing a Muslim bride all of a sudden. See what she did to her family! Who'll marry her little sister, now? She killed herself all right, but what about the ones who are left?"

I was shocked that my mother said all that. Then I heard Sati's response:

"Yes, Didi, it is sad. Such a beautiful girl, so young and she had to commit a suicide? Such a sinful act! Then, what choice did she have, Didi?"

I felt like screaming. *There was a choice. There are choices, only if you respected their love. You all messed up things for no reason. Hindus and Muslims lived together for a long time. It is possible.* But I kept quiet. The nine-point-circle theorem revolved in front of me until I shoved the book away. Meaningless geometry! I closed my eyes resting my head on my arms.

*   *   *

"*Ayee* Khuku!" Ashmani stood in front of my desk.

"You don't feel scared that I come, do you?" She gave me a side glance.

"No. Of course not, Ashmani." I assured. "At times I feel I have become you, we have merged. Believe me, Ashmani, I feel so sorry for you. So sorry that you couldn't dance that night for petty politics and I stole your show. I never told you that. You inspired me. You taught me dancing, kindled the love for dancing. And now, I feel so so sad for you!" I tried to reach her arm.

"I know that Khukumoni, I know. And that is why I come to you. Some people, even my loved ones, my own family, are scared. I scare them, but you are not scared. You invite me in your thoughts. You are strong. You are different." She replied.

"Ashmani, what strength you see in me, I don't know. I feel frustrated that I cannot speak up. I cannot stand up for all the injustice I see. I cannot protest all these nonsenses. It hurts me to hear the things they talk about you that you have no room even in heaven. I feel like screaming. But in reality, I do nothing," I sniffled.

"Don't worry for me, Khuku. It's over. I don't know about heaven or hell, I just dance around, in nothingness, in the vast abundance of nothing. I don't know how to explain it to you. But it is peaceful."

Then with a pause, she continued, "And who said I have nowhere to go? I go to those who care for me. Who makes room in their heart for me, who are not scared of me, Khuku, that's why I come to you. I will always be in your memory. I will never die as long as you keep me alive."

"I know you are not an evil spirit, Ashmani, There is nothing to be scared of you. I only wish that I were stronger. I wish I could stand up to protest what is wrong," I confided.

"I'll help you, Khuku. I will. I will stand beside you when you need me, I promise. But don't you forget to dance. Promise?" She glanced with a smile.

"Promise!" I nodded.

Ashmani disappeared. I could hear the sound of the *ghungur* from her ankles fading away.

I woke up. It startled me.

*   *   *

That night I had a strange dream that I had gone to a place up in the Himalayas. There, the River Ganga, young, swift, ran fast; the currents were strong. It was twilight time. The sun had gone down, a few stars were twinkling in the vast turquoise light.

Tiny boats floated on the river. They were made of leaves. Some had tiny lamps inside. The lighted little boats sailed with the current, dancing on the water. Some drowned, some went farther floating until they were out of my sight.

A woman was preparing her lamp. She muttered something with folded hands, like a prayer; then she gently stooped to float it on the river. Her head was covered in a shawl.

I knelt down, asked her what was she doing, what was this all about.

"*Akash pradeep (lamp to the sky),*" She answered.

"It is a way to connect with the souls that are gone, who left for the other world. This is a way to remember them, honor them, thank them for what they have done for you. This is a way to pray for them so that they are peaceful in heaven. It is a Hindu ritual, don't you know that, girl?" She looked at me. Her veil dropped. It was Ashmani!

*   *   *

After school I took the shortcut path through the woods, behind the broken masjid. This was the path that Ashmini used to take, and I had never known. This was my first time.

Strange insects and bats made eerie sounds. There was a constant susurrus, a murmur of the wind through the dense bushes. A grey bodied lizard with warty skin blocked my path. It was lunging; with front arm stretched its huge head raised up, it was staring with bulging eyes. Then it started croaking *tuck-too tuck-too* ballooning its throat. I thought this must be a *tokkhok,* which I had never seen before. A *doyel flew* by, low enough scaring the creature to run away. The indigo bird with her eggshell white belly sat on a branch near by and chirped. Doyel, her English name is Oriental magpie. Babu had taught me from his book, I remembered. While I was preoccupied with these thoughts of birds, a thin slate-colored snake zigzagged and crossed the path hiding inside a hole. I shrieked. With wider strides I started marching faster and found that the wood thinned gradually. I could see the light better. The path had gone up to a hillock and there stood a lonely *bokul* tree at the top. No other trees were around. I stood under it, panting, thinking this was where Ashmani had her first kiss that morning. This was where she was tied and whipped at the end of the day. This was the tree that had witnessed it all in silence.

Further down, a set of steps descended and merged to the riverbank. It was high tide time. Water splashed and thrusted on the steps, whirling and swirling, gushing the steps, bubbles purled.

I opened my school bag, took out my journal and snatched a page out. I folded the paper and made a paper boat. I lit a candle striking a match and crouched down to float it in the river with a prayer:

Ashmani, we never met as friends while you were alive, but I meet you every day after you are dead. I feel guilty, very guilty that I stole your show and was happy with the glory and admiration I got. You gave me a lot, you inspired me. But I had never given you anything. And I am sorry for what you had to pay for this Hindu-Musselman clash. You were innocent, you didn't deserve it. You shouldn't have died. But it happened. Now, my friend, I am here to wish you peace, so you find a place in heaven.

I stood up. Wiping my tears with the back of my hand I started to climb. Then I found myself bobbing in the water, pulled by the current. I slipped a slimy step and ended there.

"What are you doing here, in this dangerous place?" A voice shrilled. A hand pulled me up.

"It's not needed. I am fine, I can do it myself," I shrugged him off.

It was Mahim, that monda maker. He looked so different with a beard and a *musselman tupi*, I couldn't recognize him. Rahamat, his friend came forward, and the *lathial* Aziz.

"*Abhisar* (tryst) eh!" Aziz sneered, licking his lips. *Ugh!* I jerked my face away. "Tell your father to go back to your country. Go to India." Aziz remarked.

"Now your Gandhi is gone too. And he was not killed by any Musselman, mind you. Your own people murdered him that *nanga fakir (naked poor)*. Did you hear what his killer, that Hindu murderer say? What was his name? Nathuram or whatever!" He added.

"*Arre thik achhey (oh let go). Ayee meye (hey girl)*, don't you ever come here. Understand! And yes, tell your brahmin father to clutch his *paita* (sacred thread) and go to your own land, not here." Mahim shouted mocking my father clutching his thread.

I couldn't believe my ears that it was Mahim who was telling all these. Just a few years ago he was a Hindu himself, he told us the story how his father named him Aswini!

I turned and ran as fast as I could until I reached home. I thought I should tell this to Babu. But I didn't. At the end of the day, at meal time when he asked how my day went, inside I was churning, but I pretended it was just a normal day. I kept it all to myself. I continued going to school as usual avoiding that path.

*   *   *

Sounds of laughter rolled from the cafeteria. My friends, Neelofa, Lata, Shamima were giggling in merriment. I wanted to know what was this chortling all about, they must have liked the test paper much today.

"*Ayee,* how was it? Come join us." Lata invited me scooting making room for me on the bench. But before I could respond Shamima exclaimed:

"Oh, let go, let's relax for the next three free days. We'll think of tests again after that. Nilofa, what are you going to wear for the wedding party?"

"What party? Hamida's sister's wedding? Hey, how about we all wear green?" Neelofa bent forward with wide eyes.

"That's a grand idea. I can ask my ma if she'd let me wear her peridot green georgette. It's such a pretty shade you know, like the young banana leaf that has just unfurled… that beautiful hue of lime green with a touch of yellow!" Lata opened her fist, her eyes twinkled. Then she turned to me, "What about you, Khuku?"

I was not invited I realized, but before I could say anything Shamima winked at Lata and whispered in her ears, "Shh, they did not invite any Hindus."

It was strange because all these years there were several occasions when I was invited to their house, in all her sisters' weddings, during Eid festivals. Hamida had also come to our house many times with all these common friends.

"Where is Binita and Padma? I was missing them. Hope they are well." I asked.

"Padma went home early after the test, she is fine. About Binita, they have gone back to Hindustan, don't you know? All the Hindu girls, Chandra, Sabita, Ruma, they all went back to your part, in India. When are you leaving, we were wondering." Nilofa glanced at me.

"Leaving? Me? Where?" I was clueless.

"To your country, Khuku, You should also go back to your land, in Hindustan." She cleared.

"What? This is my land, Nilofa, as much as it is yours. This is my motherland. This is where I was born and grew up. This is the world I know as my home." I shouted pointing the ground with knitted brows.

"Well, not anymore, sweetie." She rotated her forefinger in front of my nose. "Calm down, dear friend, my aunt's family had to flee from Kolkata because you Hindus were torturing them to death. You shunned them out because they are Muslims. After the partition that is what is happening, Miss Khukumoni," She uttered each word at a time as if chewing the words, narrowing her eyes... "So calm down, don't you show your temper to us," Nilofa sniggered.

"I don't care. This is my home. I don't care that one day some foreign Radcliff saheb will draw an imaginary line and order me that I am ousted from my own home. I don't accept that." I stood up, pounding the table with my fist, kicking the bench, I shouted. My heart was thumping.

"Sit sit, who is Radcliff saheb, what did he do?" Lata pulled me down to sit, brushing her hands over my back asking with wide eyes. I felt comfort at the same time disgusted with Lata's innocence and peacemaking efforts.

"Go read the history, at least the newspapers, Lata," I cried.

"Look Khuku, we may not be a good student like you, we may not know who's Radcliff or whatever, but this is the simple truth we all know. There is a partition, and this is Pakistan. Professor Khukumoni, and you have to accept that." Nilofa jerked her head.

"Yes, go to Kolkata and open a school. You'll be a perfect headmistress, miss know-it-all." Shamima added.

"Uff, don't do all that to her. Come, sit, Khuku. We, I mean they don't mean all that, you see. We are friends... since class one, right? How many years, ten?" Lata tried to ease the tension.

"No, we do. At least I mean exactly what I said. No regret. You people are all like that; you Hindus, the know-it-all type, with an 'I am supreme' attitude. You people hog our best positions in offices, banks, schools, colleges. That's what my *Abba jan* (father) was saying the other day. It's true and it's enough. Now we have our own country. This is Pakistan. You go back." Nilofa was clear. "This is my land!" she mocked me thumping the table, pointing the ground and Shamima rolled over laughing.

I couldn't take it anymore. I stormed out of the cafeteria.

I felt confused as I was walking home. It started with anger, then the emotion dissolved into tears of sadness. What did I do wrong to lose them all, why did I deserve such a treatment from my close friends?

As I was passing the station road an imagery struck me, as if I was standing in front of a train track. Where the parallel lines met at a vanishing point peacefully, a gigantic engine, oblivious, was rushing in, approaching right at my face. Its fierce face looked like that of a monster's, with wide humongous eyes and exposed teeth clenched in anger. The nostrils blew fumes and smoke and it was coming to gulp me, crush me into pieces. It was coming too swiftly, with tremendous speed. I had no way to escape.

The scenario haunted me. Again and again, even when I was home. It ran over and over inside my brain. I wished I could run. Instead, I plopped on my bed, pulled the sheet and covered myself to find a safe haven.

From the other room I could hear Sati and Ma chattering, "Do you know there was an attack on the sweet meat shop next to the bus station?" Sati told Ma.

"You mean Gopal's shop? Don't we always buy our sweets from him? He is the best, always has fresh things." Ma responded.

"Yes, Gopal closed the shop. Some older boys came and demanded him to hand them all the sweets without payment. When he denied they looted his cash box and broke the glass case and hit him with a stick. He bled. That is what I heard. Now today I came to know that Gopal left with his family, to Hindustan." Sati reported.

"The Chatterjee's left last Sunday and this Tuesday the Ghosh family also went. It's not the same anymore."

Ma sighed then added, "Many of our relatives are leaving too.

They leave their homes open, unattended, left their properties just like that and are gone. Some hope to come back one day and claim for fair exchange, most do not. They take it as a loss." Ma's voice was calm but with deep sighs.

I was quite surprised that my mother was so calm and cool about this.

"I hope you are not leaving, Didi," Sati muttered.

"Actually we are Sati. We are scared too like everyone else. As soon as Khuku's tests are over we are planning to go. Khukumoni is a good student, her father thinks so. He does not want to disturb her before the exam. Matriculation examination is a big thing you know, especially for a good student. But after that we'll not stay here." Ma's voice sounded hollow.

I was shocked. No one ever told me anything about such a huge plan. It would be such a major change in our lives. My throat choked, my eyes burned. I felt like crying out loud, persuade them, convince them, cajole, whatever it took, I would kneel down and hold their hands pleading "Please don't do this. Please don't go. Please don't take me out of here."

Instead, I stayed under the cover, *This is just not happening.* I thought I rather change myself, change my own attitude. A wee voice tickled my ego that my father regarded me as a good student. He valued my education; he thought I had potential, though he had never told me so, in so many words.

I just remained motionless, eavesdropping. "I don't know, Sati, what'll happen to us. It scares me thinking of the future. Our assets were here, in this land, in this soil. That was what brought the rice on our plates at the end of the day. We were landowners. Now everything has changed. My husband never worked anywhere. No experience in that sense. We don't know anyone in Kolkata where we can start our first days. Everyone is struggling." Then with a sigh Ma added, "God will help. Something will happen."

Someone pulled my cover and a warm wet slobber brushed my forehead, my cheeks. I opened my eyes. Gypsy!

She didn't like me hiding under the cover at this hour. I sat up and caressed her under her throat. Gypsy loved this and chimed that funny noise that only Gypsy could do. *Did she understand all that Ma and Sati were talking about? Does she anticipate our separation so soon?*

I hugged her tight, and she rolled back and forth on the ground. Then she stood up. Wagging her tail in glee she lunged, pushing her front legs ready to prance. I yawned.

Gipsy tilted her head, with ears popped up she stared at me with a cooing sound. Her iolite eyes shimmered. The little white diamond on her forehead wrinkled with impatience. I kissed on that diamond on her forehead. "My Gipsy *sundari (*beautiful)! How could I leave you here, dear friend?"

She managed to squeeze her body to go under my cot and fetch the red ball. Clutching it in her mouth she brought it to me, '*Let's go play!'*

I felt much better after that vigorous run and catch game with her. An hour later when we both sat down at the steps panting, I decided to go see my friend Padma. My best friend, Padma. She'd make it all better.

* * *

And then, I saw it. From the slat gaps of the shutters in Padma's house, I saw it all.

21

SHOCK

The scene played over and over in my head like a broken record. Wished I could toss it away. I buried my face over a pillow to shut it off. But it came back. The burst of a gunshot… BANG erupting inside my head.

I wished I could cry, go run to Padma and hug her tight this very moment. At least I could go tell it to Babu . But I could do none. The shock froze me.

It shook my knees, my hands, my fingers. It dried up my tongue and my throat, choking me. I wished I could throw up. To tell it to someone. But nothing happened. An unknown fear, an emotion I didn't know what, embraced me like a python. I decided to keep quiet, not to tell anyone, not today.

"Are you sick?" Ma came and put her hand on my forehead.

"Yes, a bad headache. Tomorrow I have a test. Trying to sleep." I didn't even move my arm hiding my eyes. "Hope you don't get a fever. Rest." She drew the sheet over me, putting the light off.

That night I had a strange dream. It was that *bokul* tree where Ashmani had her first kiss and her last beating. The tree was full of blossoms. Rebati, the drummer was hanged from one of the branches, Aziz was slapping his thighs and grooming his mustache, with a nefarious grin. Uncle Kader sat in a crouched position on a rock holding his forehead, tears rolling his face. We were all around. I was in the crowd too, watching. I had never seen Uncle Kader cry. He always tried to give us strength, but this time he was a loser.

An ethereal light filled the space. Ashmani entered the stage with her shimmering yellow-rust *ghagra* dancing and twirling, singing *Pyar kiya koi chori nahi ki, pyar kiya to darna* (I loved, I didn't steal anything, I am not afraid to love). She came in front of me dancing and froze.

"You are the only hope. You are the only person who can save Rebati." She cupped her hands whispering in my ear.

"How? I am not so strong, Ashmani I have this terrible atychiphobia..." I weeped.

"What is that?"

"That is a fear, a terrible fear of failure, a fear that I am not strong enough!" I sniffled.

"Are you kidding? You're not strong? Oh! you and your big words Khuku!" She rolled her eyes. "I haven't met a girl like you, Khuku, None. Not a single one who is so soft and so strong at the same time. I'll be with you. You'll see. Just go for it." She replied.

Kakrrr kaw—a rooster crowed with the harshest shrill... *Kakrrr Kaw*. I startled. As I opened my eyes I remembered today is the big day—Math finals. This is it. This will determine my future.

*   *   *

I heard Jasimuddin entering the gate to give the newspaper to Babu.

"Something horrible happened yesterday, Sir. Dr. Kader Choudhury was killed. In his own house, in his own chamber. The murderer used a gun and Rebati, the Hindu *dhaki* was caught. Rebati was holding the gun in his hand, sitting beside the dead body. Strange.

The crowd started beating Rebati, kicking and punching, until the police came. Rebati stayed silent all along. He was taken by the police with handcuffs. Probably he will be hanged soon."

Then there was Babu's feeble, anxious voice, "Can I go see the family?"

"No Sir, the house is barricaded. Besides..." Jasimuddin hesitated.

"I understand. The Hindu-Muslim thing." Babu picked up the cue.

I went straight to take a shower to get ready for school. I did not want to face Babu. As water poured over my head, my face, my tongue, I felt much better. The water solaced me, soothed and calmed that sensation that was burning inside. It gave me an answer to what I should do today. Hiding was not the solution, not crying either.

I went to school. Finished my test, then straight to Bokul di, my favorite teacher.

"I have something very urgent to tell you, Bokul di. I haven't told it to any one. When do you have time?" Blood swarmed on my face. I stepped closer and held her arm, as I was feeling dizzy. Her eyes widened as she listened to me.

"This is so unlike you." She touched my forehead, "Are you alright? What happened to you? Let's go out right now. I have an off period." I followed her to the schoolyard under the banyan tree. Its protruded aerial roots gave me shelter like gnarled fingers of a loving old grandmother.

"Remember the Assistant District Magistrate's wife who came to see our dance performance, Bokul di? You had introduced me to her and she had said, 'Come visit me someday?' Remember? I need to visit her very soon, may be today. Can you take me or tell me how to go?" I breathed out, happy that I could say it in one breath.

Bokul di looked perplexed. "What happened? You look very disturbed. Why go to Madam? What's going on?" her brows knitted.

"I saw a horrible murder yesterday, Bokul di. Padma's father, Dr. Kader Choudhury was killed last night. He always told us to stand up for what is right. No matter how inconvenient or difficult it be. He was no less than my own father. The person who is accused is not the real culprit. I have to let the truth known before the poor man is hanged." I broke down with uncontrollable sobs. Gushes of emotion flooded inside. I felt drained.

Bokul di held me tight. She wiped off my tears and said, "Let's go right after school. I'll take you and notify your parents that you are with me. Let me see if I can find an appointment."

SHADOW BIRDS

As we entered the palatial mansion of the Assistant District Magistrate, I was greeted with a sweet smell of cake. I kneeled down to take off my shoes as that is good manners to enter someone's house. Ma taught me. I almost saw my reflection on the sparkling white marble floor.

"Don't have to take off your shoes. Just come in." The lady of the house, Madam greeted with a wide grin, climbing down the circular staircase. Her hand glided down the mahogany banister of the stair that had a snake's head carved at the very end.

She guided us to the parlor and on the way I met my face on a huge Belgium glass mirror with utter horror. My hair looked frizzy, like dried hay, flying all over my face, an angry new pimple on my chin was erupting with ferocious redness demanding immediate attention. I felt like hiding somewhere. I remembered one day she complimented me for my looks.

"Look at you! So grown up in just two years. So tall, and now you have glasses. Ready for your Matriculation test, *na*?"

I tried to smile.

"Now, what brought you here today, my child? I heard a little bit from Bokul in her message but you tell me." She said.

I took a deep breath and prayed for all the strength and then heard me saying, "Uncle Kader always taught us to tell the truth even if it was hard and inconvenient." I choked.

"Yes, yes... but who is Uncle Kader?"

"He is, he was my best friend Padma's father. He was just like my own father. I saw him being murdered yesterday." I rubbed my fingers.

"Really? Okay, go on." She was curious.

"Today I came to know that Rebati, the *dhaki* was accused as the killer and he'd probably be hanged soon. But Rebati was not the killer. I saw it all."

"Wait, wait. This is serious. My husband should hear it. Let me see if he is free." She went out of the room. The pearl white silk curtains swayed. My heart pounded faster.

"Come, my dear." She guided us to another big room. Across a huge cherry-wood table sat a gentleman with a pipe in his mouth. His salt and pepper head was almost buried in books and papers. A colossal library embraced his table with hundreds of crimson colored books with gold borders.

"Come, come, have a seat." He lifted his head and scooted back the revolving chair. Closed his thick ledger and gave a big smile.

"I am Mr. Basu. Pranab Kumar Basu. People call me P.K.. I am the Assistant Magistrate of your district. And what's your name?" He turned to Bokul di and gave her a friendly nod. I introduced myself and showed my respect with a *pranam*. He held my hand and shook it.

"Tell me what you saw. As much with all the details you can remember." He said in a baritone voice.

"I witnessed the murder of Dr. Kader Choudhury yesterday. After the sundown, I went to my friend Padma's house, his daughter. She is my best friend. Their front door, meaning the doctor's chamber was closed. I went to the back. I knew that there was an entrance but it was locked. I climbed a concrete slab to see through the window if I could draw Uncle Kader's attention. The lights were on, so he must be working, I thought.

Through the slats of the wooden shutters, I saw that Dr. Kader had two visitors in his chamber, and I recognized them both. The doctor said, 'Rebati, now what happened again?' Rebati described his stomach problem. Dr. Kader said, 'Let me give you the medicine. My helper is gone, so I have to go mix it. Just wait here.' He entered the adjoining laboratory room where he kept all his medicines. While he was mixing the potion the other man entered the laboratory." At this point, I had my panic attack again. My heart was beating fast and I started panting.

"Take your time, child. No hurry. Please give her some water." He turned to his wife. Mr. P.K. Basu took off his thick tortoiseshell spectacles and started poking at his pipe. I drank all the water and took a deep breath. I tried to visualize Ashmani. I prayed for strength and hoped this to be over soon.

Then I inhaled and started, "The man approached Uncle Kader from the back. Forcefully sat him on a chair and put a long stick across his throat. Clenching his teeth he murmured,' Troublesome facts, inconvenient truth, hmm doctor? The troubling truth is that you don't believe in our party, our endeavor, your own religion. You think your religion is just healing people, hmm?. *Shala beiman*! How do you like this troubling truth now?'

He pressed and pressed until Uncle Kader's head dropped.

That very minute Rebati, the Hindu dhaki, entered the laboratory room, and seeing this, he fainted. The other man took the red and white checkered cotton *gamchha* from his waist, unwrapped a hidden gun and shot Dr. Kader. Then he stuck the gun in Rebati's hand, opened the latch of the back room door swinging his stick, went out.

At this point I climbed down, took a rickshaw home and came through the alleyway. People heard the gunfire and I saw a crowd running to the front door of their house. Next day from our servant Jasimuddin I heard that they found the *dhaki*, Rebati with the gun in his hand and assumed that he was the killer. He's been under police custody and probably would be hanged soon. Rebati is Hindu. Everybody thinks it must be a typical Hindu-Muslim thing, that is what Jasimuddin said. But Sir, Rebati was not the murderer. It was, it was that *lathial* Aziz. I saw it all.

We are going to Hindustan soon, as soon as possible, says my father, maybe by the end of this week. So I wanted to tell this before leaving. I told this to no one else, Sir, not even my own father."

The Assistant District Magistrate sat with closed eyes. There was pin-drop silence, only the tall pendulum clock chimed tick-tock-tick-tock.

*   *   *

"You are very brave and strong, young lady." He broke the silence.
"Now, come and have some tea with us." said Madam, his wife.

The maid brought home-baked cakes. Madam poured tea for us in thin translucent china cups with gold rims. I could see the amber liquid through it. That was my first taste of tea. I thought I deserved it today. I am a grown-up lady now.

The Darjeeling tea, smelled delicate but tasted strong.

22

FAREWELL MOTHERLAND

Hiraeth (noun)—A homesickness for a home to which you cannot return, a home that maybe never was: the nostalgia, the yearning, the grief for the lost place of your past.

*   *   *

Packing started. It was time to say goodbye to my motherland. Sati and Ma were polishing the silverware. Ma brought a silver teapot close to her face, appreciating the intricate designs of vines and flowers on its spout and the base, rubbing a rag in the crevices.

"*Kee sundar* (how beautiful)." Sati drew closer.

"Never used it. Saved it for the day to serve it first to Khuku's groom, one day when he will come." Ma smiled.

"Let's have tea in it today. Now!" Babu broke out.

"No! I am cleaning and polishing to take it with us for that special day, for Khuku's wedding." Ma protested.

"We meaning? You expect me to carry a trunkful of such items with other luggage and a toddler? Are you out of your mind, Bansi?" Babu raised an eyebrow.

"Why you? There are coolies or porters to carry them, *na*?" Ma raised her eyebrow too.

"I have so much luggage, so many precious things, savings of a whole lifetime. It's not easy moving." Ma went back to her packing.

"Bansi! You don't understand. It is not just moving." Babu shook his head.

"We are approaching a future that is very different, totally unknown, unpredictable. There may not be any porter to carry our luggage. We don't know where we are going, what is that new address, or what I'll do. Things might get stolen, looted. We will have to take a train ride with all these, then change to cross the river Padma, in a ferry, Then switch to a train again to reach Kolkata. There will be no helpers. What would I do with two women and a little son?" Babu sat down with a hunched back, covering his face in his palms.

"Very well, if you don't have any idea where you are taking us, we might as well sit on top of the tin trunks and make our home." Ma sneered plopping herself on the metal box.

"That is my point. That is exactly what may happen in the beginning. Be prepared, Bansi. There are thousands of people coming to that city every day. The Sealdah station may seem violent to you. One day, I hope soon they'll take us to a P.L. Camp or somewhere permanent, and provide a roof over our head. But it may take days, weeks, months, I don't know. Until then we may have to sit just like that on the station platform. That's why my suggestion is to carry less, as little as possible." Babu sighed.

"What is P.L. Camp?" Ma's eyes widened.

"Permanent liability. Refugees!" Babu cried. "That is what we will be to the Indian Government." He added raising his voice to the next octave higher.

He must be joking. My mother would not understand the English sarcasm hidden in it. I believed the two letters stood for something else. I shivered and found that Sati had left the room.

Babu asked me if my packing was done. I showed my tote bag which I had decided to carry myself on my shoulder. Inside, I had three cotton saris for everyday wear, a favorite black and white silk one, a small soap, a toothbrush, my journal, the dictionary that Uncle Kader had given and two sharpened pencils.

"That's all?" Babu tittered shaking his head. Then, he started pacing back and forth on the long veranda, with a pensive look on his face.

Ma and Sati worked on the move. They covered the furniture with white bed sheets. The sofas, chaises, mirrors, almirahs were draped with enormous white cloths. I wondered why were they doing this? Did it make any sense to protect them from dust any more? But Ma did as if we were going to Grandfather's house and would come back in a month, like she had done other times. They looked like dead bodies.

Disgusted, I went to bed.

The morning started like everyday. Sounds of bells and conches from our temple woke me up. I got ready and went to find that Ma had cleaned the floor like any other day. She made garlands with marigold and hibiscus flowers from our garden and hung them on the idols of Radha and Krishna. The air filled with sandalwood fragrance. Lamps flickered in the dark room and the omnipresent smiles shimmered on the statues of Gods. Ma's sonorous voice rippled in *kirtan* hymns.

Then she took a long time sitting in absolute silence with her eyes closed. She stood up, closed the temple door, turned the lock and climbed down the steps.

Sati was standing at the bottom of the steps. Ma stopped and handed the key to her. Sati, perplexed, gaped at Ma's face. That stare had a lot of questions. But Ma preferred the answer to remain unspoken, fixing her eyes onto Sati, until tears started rolling down her cheeks. Sati nodded her head, biting one side of her lip, sniffling. She accepted the key and carefully tied it at the corner of her sari *anchal*.

Babu was in the garden. He was checking the back of each leaf of the rose bush for aphids and murmuring how they pester the buds. He stooped down and pulled some weeds from the vegetable garden. I remembered how he had taught me to distinguish between the carrot shoots and the good-for-nothing weeds.

What difference does it make now? Who'd eat those carrots or appreciate those roses when we were gone? Who'd take care of our garden like Babu? Would Sati really be able to open the temple door once more? Wouldn't she be scared to do that, throwing herself into idol worshipping? Wouldn't it go against her new religion?

All these flowers, lamps, fragrances would die. All those lamp holders and fragrance containers would be thrown. The precious metals and jewelry would be snatched away from our Gods and Goddesses and they would be sold for the face value of silver and precious metals. Maybe then the Gods would be taken to an auction house and a wealthy art dealer would buy it and sell it to an even richer middle man. Our beloved Radha, Krishna would end up in a foreign museum in a glass case as precious antique Hindu art pieces.

No one would love them as my Ma did, no one would sing to them at the daybreak, or confide their guilts and worries to them asking for direction. No one would know their powers. They'd lose their powers. They would stand in glass boxes, lifeless, with their omnipresent smiles!

Grown-ups think differently. They love rituals and routines. That is why they do all that. Probably routines gave them strength but I couldn't overcome my feelings, my frustrations. I felt like sinking. I felt afraid.

Finally, it was time to climb the *tonga*. Jasim da, Goffur, and Sati stood by the gate helping us with the luggage. Jasim da held Gypsy, as if he were a puppy like the day he brought him the very first time. She whimpered. Tears welled in her iolite eyes shifting in their beautiful violet and blue. *How come Gypsy understood?*

This was the first time we were traveling in a rented carriage. When Babu handed the fare money to the driver at the end, he stared at him, flabbergasted.

"I don't have change, sir." He said.

"Keep the change. Farewell." Babu picked up Ashis, my brother in one hand and Ma's bag in the other.

It seemed that the tonga driver could not believe his ears. He touched the money on his forehead, "Insallah, Mashallah! Allah bless you!" He murmured and as a way of showing his gratitude started following us, picking up the luggage and calling a coolie for us. He came all the way up to the train, helped us with the luggage and my baby brother.

The train looked normal, not like the one I had seen in the newspaper picture. We had a reserved compartment.

As we entered another traveler greeted us.

"What a surprise, Mr. Lahiri!" The man exclaimed, addressing Babu.

It was that same doctor who had stabbed the deepest wound into me establishing that I was not the real child of my parents many years ago.

"Now, who is this little boy?" He pointed to my brother.

"Our son." Ma replied.

"No! Oh what a joke! What destiny. After all these years you finally had a child of your own, But what timing! Such an inconvenient time, eh?"

The doctor stood up and locked all the doors with the iron chains and extra shackles.

"Even if you pay extra for reservation, there is no guarantee, sir. People just throng and occupy your room from every direction. They might be dropping boxes and bags through the windows. Even babies, if possible." He tried a funny smile holding the cigarette between his teeth. Then he slammed the wooden shutters. The small compartment became dark. In that darkness he started:

"It's a different world now, Mr.Lahiri. This problem with the refugees is unthinkable. You'll see that when you get down in Kolkata. Hundreds and thousands of refugees on the platform, sitting on their trunks and suitcases. Bewildered." He craned his neck and widened his eyes. Those round eyes behind his spectacles looked scary.

"Some eventually make the Sealdah Rail station their permanent home. Some go to find a relative, an acquaintance, but the relatives are stuck too, with too many homeless guests from East Pakistan, you see!

Take our case. Could I not offer you to stay in my place? But see, my hands are tied. I already have my brother-in-law's family. God knows for how long!" He rolled his eyes.

"No roof over your head, no food, no security, you will finally have to stretch your hands to accept the horrible *dole* the government is offering. In the beginning, you will not be able to eat it, but eventually, you'll get used to. And the way people get sick... I can't describe what I have seen." He shook his head.

"Men go out to seek fortune in the city. Never come back."

When is he going to stop?

The compartment felt hot and muggy. A strange musty smell overwhelmed the air. The train started moving and by and by my known world started moving away, passing me behind. The blue-gray range of the Sushong Hills, the ginger tan Brahmaputra River, the simple people I knew as my country folks and neighbors, were passing away. My past life. I raised the window pane a bit to say goodbye to my motherland, whom I might never see again. I felt a deep pang in my chest. Felt like getting down, walking to that green field and hugging that soil.

I thought of that security blanket which resembled this landscape and how it comforted me when I was little. It is torn now, shredded to pieces and I had left it. I remembered that one day I wanted to give it to Ashis as a keepsake gift.

I thought of my best friend Padma and the fact that I couldn't even say goodbye to her. She'd learn it one day that I had left, left forever, and couldn't keep my promise. I remembered how I wiped her tears, teased her for her fear, and assured I'd never leave this place.

And Uncle Kader!

*   *   *

"Khuku, can you help me with the food?" Ma whispered.

I brought the basket and the brass tiffin carrier. Ma made each of us a plate with homemade loochi, potato curry and a monda and asked me to give the first plate to our guest, the doctor.

When I handed him the plate he said, "Wait. Let me get ready." He took out a newspaper snatching it in half. One half he gave to Babu, and the other he put under his own plate.

To my utter awe, I saw a picture of Dr. Kader and a caption *The real culprit was not the dakhi* read in bold big letters.

My heart pounded. What did they find out? How did they find out? Did they mention my name? I had a million questions. But I couldn't say anything.

As I came back to my seat, looking at the vast green fields, my heart filled with a sense of joy, No one knew what I did, not even Babu, no one in my family understood what I had gone through and my huge victory today. I felt like I was Jhansir Rani, a tremendous pride and a sense of virago filled my whole self.

Then in that vast green background out the window, I saw that ethereal light again and found my dancing friend, Ashmani. I wanted to go hug her. She was the only one who knew my victory. I wanted to jump out of the window and join her in that dancing. Ashmani's uncontrollable impulse to dance, overcoming all melancholy, urged me.

The doctor stood up after finishing his meal, asked for the paper he gave to my father and crumpled them both into a ball and threw out the window. Out of the window they flew, Uncle Kader's only picture that I could have treasured and the most important news I cared for.

The doctor lit another cigarette and again clenching them between his teeth managed to shut the only window that I had kept open, with a loud thud. The room was filled with stark black darkness.

Ma put my brother down from her lap and drew me closer. I looked at her. Tears rolled down my cheeks. She wiped them and held my head closer to her bosom. After a long time, I smelled my Ma: her special body odor mixed with the smell of sandalwood soap she always used and the spices, from her kitchen. Cloves, cinnamon, cardamom. I smelled security.

SHADOW BIRDS

How come I forgot she loved me?

Ma stroked her fingers on my forehead. They were the coolest, most comforting touch. I closed my eyes. The train rumbled *dhok-a-dhok, dhok-a-dhok*, and carried me faraway as I entered into an unknown world.

*   *   *

Here, we got down at a congested platform. Coolie, coolie, shouted my father. The coolie ran so fast with our trunks and suitcases on his head that we could not keep up. We lost track of him and all our belongings were lost. We sweated and got stampeded in that choking, crushing crowd. My father collapsed holding his chest. He gasped. His face looked thin, unshaven, sick like he looked long ago when he got very ill. I tried to fan, give him water, but he closed his eyes slowly. Then he got stiff. Still.

Ma looked at me with a blank stare. I looked at her. *Is this what death is?*

*   *   *

My little brother cried. I woke up startled. Relieved, that it was only a dream, a nightmare. Babu was right there sitting across me, dozing with the rhythmic thud of the train.

"Babu!" I whispered. He opened his eyes and smiled.

I pulled up the window shutter closest to me. Aurora. The hour before dawn, in Bengali it is called the *Brahmo Muhurto*. Uncle Kader had told us it was the most auspicious time of the day. The most precious, promising one. The most beautiful hour. Our train was coming out of a tunnel and I could see the sunrise.

Like a red ball, it sprung up on the horizon tearing all darkness of the night.

ACKNOWLEDGEMENTS

This book would not be written had my mother not told me the stories of her childhood with utter frankness and nostalgic details, and about the agony she felt for the partition in the name of freedom.

This book would not be written if my writer father had not nudged me—"Write only if you can't do without." It haunted me more after they both passed away, and I felt compelled to write this story.

I am lucky to have a husband who is the first reader of all my works, from the very first draft to the finished version. His yawns direct me that it needs to be rewritten, and his helpful comments perk me up when I am lazy or numb with writer's block. His sharp eyes for details helped in final editing.

Thank you for your patience Amit, when I appeared absent-minded, and understanding the fact that actually, I was then writing in my head. Thank you for putting up with those burned dinners because I had a rare unexpected visit from the muse.

I count my blessings for finding Jil Plummer at the right time at the California Writers Club. That day I was new and she invited me to sit next to her. I was looking for an editor, a critique group and some good writer friends. She provided them all. Thank you, Jil for editing my book with so much care and thoughtfulness.

I am grateful to all the writer friends in our close-knit critique group for supporting me in this journey. Margie Witt, Wendy Blakeley, Ken Kerkhoff, and Bill McGinnis, I appreciate your valuable feedback and support.

Wayne Neel and Gretchen Davis, I can't thank you enough for being my beta readers and taking the time reading the entire manuscript so very thoroughly and giving me precious suggestions. I have implemented many.

This is a work of fiction. Characters and events are imagined. Yet, several stories, songs, photographs and books fueled my imagination. I must mention the Bengali memoir 'Jiboner Indradhonu' written by Dr. Dhriti Kanto Lahiri Choudhuri. I would like to express deep respect for him. Heartfelt thanks to the victims of the partition who participated and told their stories in the Oral History of India's Partition Project.

Throughout the last fourteen years of writing this book, I had taken several writing classes and joined many writers' groups. I am grateful to those writer friends for their comments and confidence in me; especially Ellen Starkman and late Roy Kahn.

Sharon Stewart, thank you for your interest in my writing, and reading it in the very initial stage when I was doubtful. Your editing help and the confidence in my work were what I needed desperately at that time. I must include Antara Basu-Zych for reading it in that initial stage and critiquing.

Nina Basu Nulman, thank you for reading it all the way and the important questions you asked, and Boris Nulman, for crossing the 't's and dotting the 'i's so very meticulously.

Finally, Andrew Benzie, thank you for putting it together for a fledgling writer, sharing your experience and helping with those little details from designing the book cover to publishing with finesse.

ABOUT THE AUTHOR

Anindita Basu is a writer from Walnut Creek, a quaint suburb near San Francisco, where she raised her family and lived for more than forty years. Born and brought up in Calcutta, India, she writes and publishes her works regularly in both languages—her mother tongue Bengali and English.

Retired from her teaching career, Basu now immerses herself in writing, and is an active member of the California Writers Club. When the muse abandons she fiddles with beads. She also loves to plan to travel with her husband to far away places.

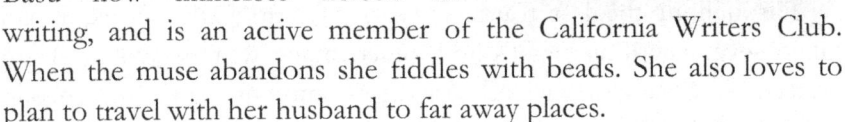

Her new book, a contemporary women's fiction, *Dreamcatcher: Story of an immigrant Bride from India* is coming soon. It is written under her pen name Dita Basu. To know more or chat with her drop her a line at www.ditabasu.com/contact/.

If you have read *Shadow Birds* please leave a review. It took her fourteen years to write it and your feedback will keep her motivated to write more. She'd love to keep in touch with you. Check her out at www.Ditabasu.com.

You may also find her in Facebook under Anindita Basu writer.

Part of the proceeds go to www.womenforwomen.org.